OA

Justin Charles Mason

Copyright © 2018 Justin Charles Mason

All rights reserved. No part of this book may be reproduced or transmitted in any form or by any electronic or mechanical means, including photocopying, recording or by any information storage and retrieval system, without the written permission of the Author, except where permitted by law.

Published by Sausage Fingers Publishing ©2018

Book Cover Design by Charley Whittingham
c/o https://m.facebook.com/BertifulMUA/

Back cover photograph by Hannah Louise Proctor (used with kind permission)
Book edited by author 2018

ISBN:9781729083413

SAUSAGE **FINGERS**
Publishing

THIS COLLECTION OF SHORT STORIES IS A COMPLETE WORK OF FICTION. ALL NAMES, CHARACTERS, BUSINESSES, PLACES, EVENTS, LOCALES, AND INCIDENTS ARE EITHER THE PRODUCTS OF THE AUTHOR'S IMAGINATION OR, AS IN THE CASE OF CHARD, USED IN AN EXTREMELY FICTITIOUS MANNER. ANY RESEMBLANCE TO ACTUAL PERSONS, LIVING OR DEAD, OR ACTUAL EVENTS IS PURELY COINCIDENTAL.

CONTENTS

1	LAYLA	Pg 1
2	OLD SCHOOL	Pg 13
3	THE WALL	Pg 29
4	MEMORIES FADE	Pg 49
5	HEAVEN OR HELL	Pg 67
6	BLESS HER COTTON SOCKS	Pg 81
7	THE BIKE DEAL	Pg 99
8	ALONE	Pg 111
9	FROM THE INSIDE	Pg 129
10	'TIS THE SEASON	Pg 143

LAYLA

She was seated at a small table at the back of the coffee shop, her eyes on the small paperback she held in slender fingers, a thin book with a picture on the cover of a man on a beach, with an umbrella. It was called 'On The Outside', which I recognized as written by a guy that lived nearby. I'd read it and although the twist was original, it stopped before it had really got going.

She seemed to be enjoying it though and at least it could be a pretty good topic as an opening for a conversation.

If I could summon up the courage to even approach her.

For some reason, even at my relatively young age I struggled to find the bravado that many of my friends possessed, apparently being tall, dark and fairly handsome wasn't enough to make me that confident. Most of my friends used to laugh at my inability to talk to strangers, let alone strange women that frequented coffee shops but I was alone this time and I took a deep breath and walked slowly forward.

My courage had suddenly found itself. It was in the back there, cowering in the semi-darkness, next to self-doubt and disbelief and had decided to make a break for it, giving the finger to the rest of my cowering characteristics.

My mouth was dry as Jesus' flip-flop, my palms as sweaty as a nun in a cucumber patch but I swallowed hard and made my way over to her table, my eyes never leaving her down-turned face.

She was sat there in Levi 501's and a dark, Foo Fighters t-shirt, her brown, leather, bomber jacket draped over the comfortable chair opposite, her feet, encased in black, ankle-high, calf-skin boots, tapping to a beat only she seemed able to hear. Her lengthy, blazing red hair was tied back in a loosely-tied pony-tail, black Emporio Armani reading glasses perched precariously upon her smallish nose, a wry smile on her thin, red lips.

From a distance, her eyes seemed to be as blue as the deepest, clearest ocean but as I approached her, and they rose from the page to fall on mine, I could see they were, what you would probably class as mint green. Hardly poetic and romantic but they were the palest eyes I had ever seen in my life.

The soft smile on her lips never faded as she looked up at me and I could have sworn her eyes flashed mischievously as I stood before her, trying hard not to come across as some stammering, stuttering school-boy, I tried not to belie my fear and trepidation.

"Don't take this the wrong way," I started, "but could I buy you a coffee?"

Immediately I wanted the ground to swallow me

whole, almost feeling the ground starting to fall away beneath my feet.

"How could I take that the wrong way?" she replied, her smile becoming wider, the laughter lines around her eyes and her petite nose crinkling adorably, "unless you have dishonourable intentions?"

I could feel the warm flush of embarrassment crawling up my throat as I stood there fidgeting, feeling my balls tighten involuntarily at the sound of her soft, warm, slightly husky voice.

I opened my mouth to protest my innocence, proclaim I only wanted to buy her a coffee, possibly tell her I was sorry to have troubled her.

She continued to smile and let out a throaty but brief chuckle, her eyes fixed upon mine with what looked like fiery determination.

I could have sworn I could see the tip of her tongue flick out of the corner of her mouth before she spoke once again;

"I'm kidding," she laughed, "don't look so serious."

I hadn't realized I was. I thought I was just looking petrified.

She motioned for me to sit down with her, picking up her leather jacket from the seat next to her, then signalled the waitress who was loitering near the service area, looking bored and eager to finish her shift.

The woman sat opposite me was called Layla and when I had first learnt of her name, all I could think about was Eric Clapton.

Eric was Derek of Derek & The Dominoes whose seminal seventies rock song, with possibly the most anthelmintic opening guitar salvo of all time, was Layla. As that song was inspired by the 12th-century Persian poet, Nizami Ganjavi's 'The Story of Layla And Majnun' and Clapton's as-then unrequited love of Pattie Harrison, wife of Beatle George, it seemed quite apt that it was her name.

And I was suitably obsessed.

I had first seen Layla at Oakleigh's gym, "Move It To Lose It", situated off the town's Main Street, a five-minute walk from the "Welcome Home" coffee shop/café I currently found myself in.

She had been on the treadmill, in black, Lycra leggings and a 'Frankie Says Relax' t-shirt, iPhone ear-buds in, covered in a thin film of sweat and smiling that perfect smile as she pounded away like a demented long-distance runner.

And of course, it had been her bouncing boobs that had first caught my attention.

Hey, I am shallow, but I would be the first to admit it to anyone who'd be bothered to find out what made me tick. Got to be upfront with these kind of things as lying gets you nowhere.

Apparently.

I had been too embarrassed by a) my own poor physical condition b) my obvious interest in her chest, to actually approach her at that time but since then, I'd been a little more discreet when watching her and through various, slightly underhand means, I had learnt more about her.

Say what you like about social media, but it has its uses. Albeit in a freaky, creepy and ultimately quite weird way. People post far too much online. And people exploit it.

Sad, lonely, pathetic losers who are fascinated

with holiday snaps, selfies, pictures of nights on the town and intimate details spread out for all to see.

Layla wasn't the loser.

That was me. And I never said I was one of the 'good guys'.

I had found out that she was in her early 30's, lived alone with two cats, liked rock music and Pink Gin, had been engaged to a meat-head, muscle-bound dickhead named Cory. She worked as a commodity's broker over in nearby Taunton, she loved to cycle and visit the coast, she had a thing for tattoos and beards and loved to change her hair colour as much as most people changed their socks.

Layla considered herself kind, caring, a little brash, a LOT more vocal than most, swore like a blue-collar docker with Tourette's and always saw the good in everyone, no matter how big an actual arsehole they really were.

I was her perfect match.

She smiled at me as I sat down beside her, her eyes flashing mischievously (or so I believed at the time) as the young waitress sauntered over and in a loud voice, gave the little Missy her order.

Layla ordered me a tall latte, which warmed me no end, being my beverage of choice, I knew instantly that we were going to get along like a house on fire.

"I have a confession to make," Layla sighed as the girl brought over the coffees and went back to leaning bored against the counter, "I know your face, but I can't remember where the fuck I know you from."

She grinned that gorgeous smile at me and I melted some more.

"We go to the same gym," I replied, trying my

hardest not to let my eyes gaze wander from her eyes, to her full lips, to the curve of her slender chin and downwards, "but I've seen you around."

"You a stalker?" Layla laughed.

"Oh, definitely," I replied, trying to stay cool, calm and collected at the thought of my pouring over her pictures and posts being construed as being 'stalker-ish', "bit of a serial killer on the quiet too."

Layla laughed yet again and for a split second, I found myself wondering if she ever didn't laugh? Did she ever break down and cry? Did she ever hate something so bad that she'd shiver in furious anger?

I somehow doubted it.

"Well at least that's out in the open. I'll warn my friends to question you, if I suddenly disappear."

She ran a hand through her tousled hair and gave me a comical wink, sipping from her coffee cup.

"So, Mr. 'I'm-Going-To-Murder-You-In-Your-Sleep', tell me some more about yourself," she said, raising one eyebrow quizzically, "cos you seem like a nice guy, but you've got me worried now."

I proceeded to tell her about myself, trying desperately not to give too much away as I'd been told, or read somewhere, that women liked men to be all mysterious, not to let them know absolutely everything.

Maybe that was the reason at the age of 35, I was single, hadn't had a date in about eighteen months and had taken to obsessing over women I'd never talked to, let alone met properly.

Anyway, I told Layla about my job as a freelance reporter for The Oakleigh Herald, covering the sports in and around the local area and she seemed genuinely interested, even maybe slightly impressed. The newspaper had a much bigger readership than The Chard & Ilminster newspaper that covered more towards those two nearby towns and the abomination that was Crewkerne, The Oakleigh Herald was more Oakleigh-centric and was only fortnightly and occasionally incorporated what the Chard newspaper was reporting.

It wasn't a glamorous job, by any stretch of the imagination and if I was completely honest hardly ANYTHING happened in Oakleigh, it was the quintessential, quaint, small Somerset town that sensationalism seemingly forgot.

Layla was enthralled though.

I couldn't believe my eyes, she was nodding and smiling, leaning in as I spoke, almost hanging on my very word.

She seemed quite happy when I told her that I lived alone in a small flat not far from the Hangman's Arms public house and that there hadn't been anyone significant for quite a while now.

I suddenly realised it was probably mock-appreciation of what I was being said, I was making the school-boy error of spending the whole time talking about myself, instead of her.

Damn, I was out of practice.

"Anyway, enough about me," I blustered, feigning mock indignation, "let's talk about you. What do you think of me?"

This made Layla laugh out loud, her guffaw filling the rather quiet café.

"You're a funny guy!" she giggled, "and I can't for the life of me, figure out why there's no girlfriend in your life?"

"Don't forget, I murder women in their sleep!" I

laughed.

Layla nodded in agreement, her smile never fading.

"Ah yes, the Oakleigh Herald's mild-mannered reporter by day, Jason Voorhees by night."

"I was always partial to Michael Myers myself," I replied, finishing my coffee, "loved that mask."

"William Shatner," Layla said, winking knowingly, "see, I'm quite a geek really. I'm full of useless information like that."

I was already smitten, finding out that this gorgeous woman, with that cheeky smile, warm eyes and a body to die for, was a trivia aficionado, was the icing on the cake. I knew that the mask Mike Myers wore in the Halloween movies was a rubber William Shatner mask painted white and the fact she knew the same was rather endearing.

"So," Layla sighed, "do we get another coffee or cut through all this bullshit and get the fuck out of here?"

If I hadn't already finished my drink, I would have choked on my coffee or spat it unceremoniously across the room. As it was, all I could do was hope my eyes hadn't widened too wide in astonishment or my mouth had fallen open as my jaw fell on the floor.

"I know a place we can go." she said quietly, rising from her seat and slipping on her leather jacket, her green eyes never leaving mine as I rose unsteadily to my feet.

"It's a little bit of a walk, but as it's a nice sunny day, we can talk some more as we go."

I was intrigued. And a little steadier on my feet as we made our way out of the café, blinking like newborns as we stepped out into the June sunshine.

The street was full of people out enjoying the glorious weather. Shoppers bustled around; mothers with children in tow using pushchairs like battering rams, middle-aged couples, hand in hand, o their weekly shops, teenagers milling around and loitering in the town centre.

All of them oblivious to my knocking knees, sweaty palms and nervous gait as I walked alongside Layla, her hair bouncing with each graceful, yet purposeful step, literally blinded by her beauty.

"You look nervous," Layla laughed with a girly giggle that was both endearing and childish in equal measure, "you have nothing to worry about."

As she placed a reassuring hand on my forearm, I could have sworn I literally felt electricity pass between us as she led me across the busy Main Street, up away from the centre, up the steep curve of the hill.

The outskirts of the town fell away as we walked and talked, the pair of us walking over the small bridge that straddled the river, making our way out into the gorgeous, green countryside.

"Where are we actually going?" I asked as Layla peeled off her leather jacket, her dark t-shirt tightening around her torso as she threw back her head and laughed.

"Blackman Woods." She replied.

Realisation crawled up my spine as a cool chill buffeted the pair of us, I couldn't tell whether it was an actual chill in the air or the thought of those damn woods. Blackman Woods had a reputation as a meeting place for cheating couples and as the final resting place of a poor young woman, found dead in the clearing by the ruined chapel and a former police officer who'd hung himself.

And apparently there were more bodies found there throughout the years.

But if Layla was superstitious or wary, it didn't show as she led me up the lanes out of the town, the two of us taking the side lane that led up to the hill, its small car-park and the woods. She talked animatedly about the town, the weather, the haunted chapel and then as we made our way to the small signpost for the public footpath that snaked up through the woods, she started talking about me.

She asked me about my last girlfriend, Josie.

It dawned on me that I'd never mentioned Josie as we walked through the arch of over-hanging trees and up the darkened path.

Then she took my hand and I could have sworn her fingers were icy cold as they laced with mine, her head resting on my shoulder as she pulled me close and made the walk rather awkward.

Then she mentioned Olivia and Steph, my two previous girlfriends and I could feel my spine literally tingle.

I stopped in my tracks, took a step back and placing both of my hands on her shoulders, I turned her to face me.

She still smiled, almost demurely, up at me, her once green eyes now flecked with blue and I could have sworn red.

"I have another confession to make," Layla said softly, and I could have sworn she was going to start singing 'Best of You' by the Foo Fighters.

If the words "I'm no fool" came out of her mouth, I could have sworn I would burst out laughing.

They didn't.

"I know a lot more about you than I've been letting on," Layla continued, that plastered-on smile becoming slightly unnerving, "I've been following you for months now. Facebook stalking you, learning all about you, trying desperately to pluck up the courage to speak to you."

I looked incredulously at her, a confused smile spreading across my face, tilting my head like some intelligent collie trying to understand a command.

"I d-d-don't understand," I stammered, feeling the flush of embarrassment rising up from the pit of my stomach, threatening to choke the words from me at my reddening neck, "why?"

Layla looked up at me, her smile fading slightly, her eyes full of what I took to be shame though it could have been affection, I was never any good at reading women's eyes, expressions or anything if I was honest.

It was then I felt a small scratch upon the top of my hand and yelping slightly, looked to and saw that Layla had unceremoniously stuck me with a hypodermic needle.

She giggled a rather sinister sounding laugh and leaned forward, placing a warm, tender kiss upon my open mouth.

I could feel my eyes widen in shock as a cold, numbing sensation started to flood up from my pierced hand, up my arm, my shoulders, spreading across my entire torso.

"Pretty soon you will pass out, my love," Layla purred, softly stroking my cheek as she gazed up at me, pressing herself against my tightening chest, "but don't worry, you won't feel a thing."

I opened my mouth to speak as the coldness clawed at my throat, feeling the numbness take hold of my faltering body, the words failing to materialize as I stumbled backwards against what I realized was the infamous Hanging Tree, at the entrance to the clearing of the ruined chapel.

Layla let me go and I could feel everything become numb as I slid down the gnarled tree trunk, the only thing I could use was my eyes as she laid her leather jacket down and pulled her t-shirt from the waistband of her jeans and up over her head.

All I could do was watch as she slid down her jeans and stepped out of them, standing before me in matching black underwear, curvaceous, slender and looking for all the world like a centrefold model in a woodland photo-shoot.

"But," she said softly as she bent down to retrieve something from the inside pocket of her jacket, "you will be able to feel everything."

It was then I saw the knife.

"You realise," she continued, stepping slowly toward me, that unnerving smile widening, "I love you that much that no one will ever take you away from me. And I don't want you to live without me."

She bounced with every step and if I could have said anything I would have said that I was scared stiff, if I could actually say or feel anything.

The scream I gave out was a silent one.

OLD SCHOOL

Oakleigh Comprehensive, sitting on the southern edge of the town, nestled within the rather unflattering setting of the town's biggest trading estate, definitely wasn't the most glamorous of schools, but it was a good school, nonetheless. It hadn't been elevated to Academy status, like Holyrood in nearby Chard, mainly because the board of governors weren't as forward thinking, or more accurately, didn't have ideas above their station. Oakleigh itself was quite a bit smaller than Chard but the schools were virtually the same size, Oakleigh Comprehensive built ten years later so wasn't quite as run-down and slightly less dilapidated. Or had such a bad reputation.

This was mainly in part, thanks to the headmistress Pamela Stephens.

She was an American ex-patriot, living for the past twenty years in England, formerly from New York State. A certified force-of-nature who was loved by all that knew her, a wild spirit who had the greatest affection for all children, she was loved by the parents, the board of governors and most importantly, all the children she encountered.

Ms. Stephens was a diminutive woman, no more than

five feet tall, aged somewhere between 50 and 60, so far no one had been able to ascertain her actual age. She was always seen in some dodgy, retro kaftan, usually tie-dyed some psychedelic colours, her long, straggly, white hair always down around her shoulders. She wore thick-rimmed, horned glasses that always reminded everyone of some old crone in a 50's High School movie.

But she was no crone.

She was as sharp as a tack and as bright as a button.

As she always told anyone who would listen.

She never suffered fools gladly, never had the wool pulled over her eyes, always had a good word about everyone, even the hard-nosed teachers in her employ, that everyone else hated. She rarely had to raise her voice, her calming, soothing tones could diffuse any blazing row, any vocal disagreements, any jumped-up, pumped-up teenager with anger issues.

Admittedly, Oakleigh Comp was lucky that the majority of pupils came from Oakleigh and the surrounding villages, as Chard, Ilminster and Crewkerne, all nearby, were a little more 'rough and ready'. There was no uniform enforcement which, although the governors had tried to make Pamela enforce when she took over the role, she had vehemently disagreed and fought them tooth and nail.

Naturally, she had won, though as was typical of her, she never made a song and dance about it, she always maintained that if she was left alone to run the school as she felt fit, then there would never be any problems.

Up until now, she was correct.

When Jeremy Masters, Oakleigh Comp's P.E teacher upped sticks and left the town without warning, seemingly disappearing into thin air, Pamela had advertised for his replacement through the usual avenues but hadn't been able to find one candidate willing.

Until Deborah Sheldon turned up in the school

reception that early Monday morning.

Pamela's secretary Katherine, was always the first person she saw every morning, always greeted her with a cheery smile and a piping hot cup of black coffee as she walked through the school's entrance, the hiss of the electric, sliding double doors heralding Pam's arrival.

But this particular morning, Katherine was chatting animatedly to a black-haired, tall woman who was sat in one of the reception's chairs and didn't look up until Pam coughed to signal she was there.

The woman was dressed impeccably in a black pinafore dress over a white blouse, her dress matching perfectly the colour of her cropped hair with a swept over fringe that, as Pamela in her mind, made her think of Carly Simon; dipped strategically below one eye. Pamela was slightly disappointed that there was no apricot-coloured scarf but knew it would have ruined the ensemble. And this woman was definitely not craggy, old Warren Beatty.

Sat on the woman' lap was a black, leather briefcase that looked like the old 'clutch-purse style' prevalent in so many American movies, that immediately endeared the woman to Pamela and she smiled warmly as the woman turned her head to look up at her.

Her eyes were dark, almost black but Pamela could have sworn that they were cobalt-blue for an instant. The woman's smile was almost as bright, perfect, white teeth almost dazzling as she looked up at her, perfectly complimented by the blood-red lipstick worn upon her full lips.

There were a few lines on the woman's face, small crow's feet at the corner of the eyes but she was one of those women that you had no idea of what age they were; if Pamela had to guess, she would have put her at late thirties, possibly early forties. She wore very little make-up but still looked radiant. She wore no jewellery, no earrings, no wedding band.

Pamela was smitten.

There was a rumour throughout the school that Pamela preferred the company of ladies, rather than men and in these times of gender-equality, gender variance and LGBTQ, no one judged her in the slightest.

But Pamela had never truly revealed where her loyalties or in fact, where she lay but if anyone had asked her at that precise time, she would have said she had fallen for this dark-haired, stunning woman.

Katherine finally noticed her employer standing in front of them and becoming slightly flustered and red-faced, beamed that lop-sided smile of hers and brushed her frizzy, brown hair from her eyes.

"Oh, Pamela, I'm so sorry, I didn't see you there!" she stammered, her thick Somerset accent cutting through the silence of the reception, "this is Deborah Sheldon."

The woman rose and outstretched her hand.

"Debbie, Debbie Sheldon," she said with a blossoming smile as she took Pamela's hand and shook it vigorously, "I'm her for the teacher vacancy."

Pamela couldn't place her accent, but she could have sworn there was an underlying hint of an American twang beneath the perfectly clipped, upper-class, English accent.

"You teach P.E?" Pamela replied, marvelling at the softness of the woman's skin and the firmness of her grip.

"Amongst other things," Debbie retorted, flashing what Pamela perceived to be a mischievous grin, "I'm a jack-of-all-trades."

It turned out that Deborah Sheldon was indeed multi-talented, well experienced with a career in teaching going back twenty-five years and incredibly, was closer to fifty than forty. According to her CV, she had done her teacher training at Bath Spa University and had majored in Math's, English, French and Physical Education. She had served her apprenticeship in a prestigious finishing school in London and for the past twenty years had worked in France, Switzerland, Vietnam, Japan, Canada and America.

But, she was an Oakleigh girl, born and bred in this very town. There was no family left, no significant other. She lived alone in an old cottage on the northern side of the town, a private-rented property that backed onto the Blackman Woods and Richards Hill with the infamous ruined chapel sat on top, hidden within the ring of trees. There was a cat, apparently the only companion that Deborah bothered sharing her life with.

She had settled into her position as P.E teacher with consummate ease, apparently well liked by her pupils instantly, especially those hormonally-charged fifteen-year old boys, which no one on the teaching staff was particularly surprised at. It had become the topic of the staffroom gossip on a seemingly daily basis, the teaching faculty, numbering only about ten, were all captivated with this dusky, softly spoken woman with the deep, pool-like eyes and cheek bones that looked like they'd been chiselled out of porcelain.

English teachers, Tom Oliver and Alan Parsons were vying for Deborah's affections, at an almost embarrassing level, literally falling over themselves to fawn over her, hanging on her every word like love-sick teenagers with their puppy-dog eyes and their salivating tongues out.

Deborah never gave them the time of day.

She was never rude but she gave off this aura of aloofness that made the two men want her even more. She would just smile demurely to herself, never meet their gaze, seemingly stare off into the distance as if searching for something beyond.

About a month into Deborah's tenure, at the end of October, Pamela found Deborah waiting outside her office, one Tuesday morning, sat alongside a fifteen-year old boy, Will Richards. It was after the lunchtime bell had rung for the children to return to class and Pamela looked quizzically at the pair of them, knowing they should both be in classes.

"Tom Oliver is watching my class," Deborah said

coldly, seemingly knowing what Pamela was thinking, as she rose from her chair, standing almost defiantly before the diminutive headmistress, "this matter is rather urgent Ms. Stephens."

"You'd better come in." Pamela sighed, nodding to Katherine, sat at her desk outside, "Kate, hold all my calls."

Katherine nodded her response and looked stern, as if this was a usual occurrence and solemnity was the norm.

It wasn't.

Pamela shut the door behind them as Deborah and Will sat in two chairs and Pamela rounded her teak desk and sat reluctantly in her soft, padded, leather chair to look at the pair before her.

Deborah was wearing her obligatory white and red Nike tracksuit over a white t-shirt, the outfit she was normally found in most school days that reminded those of a certain age, of Lt. Callahan in the Police Academy movies. If she dyed her hair blonde and wore mirrored sunglasses then she would have been a dead ringer.

Will Richards was wearing a plain black t-shirt and faded, blue denim jeans, his hair shoulder-length, his eyes as blue as the crisp October sky outside the large office window. He was considered to be a handsome lad, a little moody but with a quip and a smile that apparently endeared him to most females, even the teachers.

But apparently, not Deborah Sheldon.

"I am sorry to bring this to you," Deborah sighed, her face expressionless as she stared into Pamela's eyes, without blinking, "but this is quite a serious matter."

Pamela, slightly unnerved by Deborah's stare and demeanour, looked backwards and forwards at the pair sat before her, Will's gaze was lowered, staring intently at his hands that fidgeted awkwardly in his lap.

"I caught Mr. Richards here, at the beginning of the lunch period," Deborah started, her eyes upon Pamela, not acknowledging Will's presence next to her, "he was writing obscene statements upon his tutor-room whiteboard, alongside to a printed photograph of a naked woman, with my head superimposed upon it."

Pamela raised an eyebrow, fixing Will with a steely glare that she hoped displayed her disapproval accordingly.

"Do you have any explanation for your behaviour young man?" Pamela asked sternly.

Will sat there, shoulders hunched, still looking rather sheepish, not daring to utter a word in his defence.

"Go and sit outside while I discuss the matter with Miss Sheldon."

Once the two women were alone, Pamela dropped her 'angry headmistress' bearing and sighed.

"I want him severely punished," Deborah snorted, "what he wrote & the utter filth upon that board sickened me. I've never been so humiliated in all my life."

Pamela thought that Deborah was possibly overreacting slightly, she obviously never had much experience of hormonally-excitable, teenage boys, which surprised Pamela, as Deborah's CV had listed numerous schools where she surely would have.

"What would you suggest?" Pamela said with a sigh, deciding against any sort of smile with the pure ire etched upon Deborah's face, staring back at her.

"I'd string the dirty little bastard up by his dick." Deborah spat, her eyes narrowing as she growled.

Pamela was internally and almost visibly shocked.

This was the first time Deborah had displayed any kind of real emotion and it surprised the hell out of Pamela. Deborah had done nothing but smile demurely since the first time she'd met her, barely raising her voice from a whisper for most of the time they had spoken.

Pamela was alarmed by the change in her but kept a cool, level-headed approach as always.

"Surely you've had some experience with horny school boys?"

Deborah's silence and equally stony stare said

otherwise.

Keeping her smile short, Pamela leant on her elbows upon the desk, resting her chin on the tips of her fingers.

"We'll start with a month of detention and a strongly worded letter to his parents-"

"I have a better idea," Deborah interrupted, "cane the little shit."

Pamela felt her mouth fall open but couldn't help herself falling forward, slipping off her supporting fingers.

"Chrissakes Deborah," she gasped, "want me to string him up from the longest yard-arm? Get the 'Cat-o-Nine-tails' and give him fifty lashes? We're a little more progressive and forward-thinking these days, we've moved on since the Middle Ages."

Deborah's icy stare didn't change but Pamela could have sworn that she heard a little growl from within her throat, feint but there nonetheless, menacing and a little unsettling.

Composing herself, Pamela leaned back in her leather chair and laced her fingers behind her head, sighing once more.

"OK," she continued softly, "I'm sure you are aware we desperately need to clear out the equipment shed behind the swimming pool, how's about I get Will to do it as part of his punishment? I am sure his parents wont mind him staying behind after school every day this week."

"I take it you would like me to supervise?" Deborah retorted, snorting dismissively, "I have some good ideas when it comes to workloads."

Pamela found herself hoping that they were slightly less archaic or barbaric as her teaching ideas.

For the children's sake.

As the week progressed, it seemed that Deborah seemed to have trouble with pupils, virtually daily. Will Richard's was the first of five male students that had invoked her fury as four others had been caught vandalizing, graffiting, fighting and one even arguing with her.

Pamela found her sat outside her office each day, her once smiling features seemingly etched into a mask of contempt and resentment. She had been told by most of the staff that came into contact with Deborah that she was cold, unresponsive and even downright rude on some occasions.

By the time Tim Gower was sat in Pamela's office, on that Friday, explaining why he had carved in Deborah's desk 'Miss Sheldon is a bitch' with a Swiss Army Knife, Pamela decided she would get to the bottom of this.

After asking Tim to wait outside and shutting the door behind him, Pamela sat on the corner of her desk and faced Deborah, today wearing a black polo-shirt and black Adidas tracksuit-bottoms with the two white striped down the leg. Deborah's hair was slicked back, close against her head and she wore the face of someone not right with the world.

"Deborah, I'm concerned," Pamela sighed, toying with the multi-coloured beads that matched her kaftan, "while i do not doubt that these young men have a serious problem with you at the moment, I can't help but wonder if there is something going on that i should know about."

Deborah looked up at her, the corners of her lips turning up slightly as a small, wry grin spread across her face.

"It seems like I've become a magnet for the juvenile delinquents in this year," Deborah replied, with a derisive scoff, "i don't know what I've done to deserve all this negative attention and to be honest, downright obscene persecution."

"Do you actually have any of these students in your lessons?"

Deborah shook her head.

Pamela went back around her desk and sitting in her

chair, took out a notepad with a list of the boy's names from one of her desk's deep drawers. She looked down at the list, noticing that the four already on the list were all, what the Americans would call 'straight-A students' and had never shown any bad behaviour in the past. Yet all of them had made a bee-line for Deborah, had written obscenities about her, all over her office and the school, had shown a blatant hatred for her and Pamela was confused as they come.

"I don't know what the answer is," Pamela sighed, "i thought all the students were extremely fond of you."

Deborah never said a word, just kept staring at her with those dark eyes, her lips pursed, her stoic hands in her lap.

"I should probably mention that the equipment shed is a mammoth task," Deborah said, rather robotically, "I will need the five boys to help tomorrow also."

Pamela hesitated, she wasn't sure a Saturday Club was the best idea for a punishment, they weren't in California and Simple Minds would not be playing over their end credits.

"I'll have to run it past the governors, post haste," Pamela said softly, "it's most irregular."

Deborah nodded slowly.

"Send Tim back in and I'll let you know by 3pm what the answer is."

Pamela watched Deborah rise from her chair and make her way to the door, trying desperately not to watch her shapely backside as she walked away, and as equally desperately trying to figure out what the hell had tipped these boys over the edge. Tim Gower entered the office, still looking as sheepish and as his eyes met Deborah's as he passed, Pamela thought that for an instant there was more than distaste there, as anyone would have expected.

It was more like adoration.

Pamela made Tim sit and looked over her horn-rimmed glasses at him, regarding him before she spoke.

He was a thin lad, fair-skinned and fair-haired, wore plain, National Health glasses and looked far too small for the shirt and trousers he wore. He wasn't a particularly bright student, not athletically astute, nothing special about the boy at all. He was usually a quiet boy, kept himself to himself and didn't have a lot of friends.

In fact, he was exactly the same as the four other boys in that respect.

All of them were Oakleigh boys.

Then she realised they were all farmer's sons.

And all were descendants of the town's founding fathers: Richards, Jameson, Thomas, Williams and finally Gower, the five men who had written the town Charter four hundred years previous.

Pamela, dismissed the notion as quick as it arrived, laughing internally at the absurdity of it.

Everyone in Oakleigh was descended from those five families, hell, she was surprised there weren't more cases of webbed-feet, six toes, mental and physical abnormalities with all the in-breeding apparently prevalent in the town.

She proceeded to tear Tim a new one, in the nicest way possible.

After all, she didn't have the reputation as a bitch and wasn't about to cultivate that particularly unwanted predilection, any time soon.

Pamela drove through the school gates the following morning, her Fiat trundling noisily through to the car-park at a little after eleven-thirty. The place was as deserted at the trading estate she passed through and she was surprised that she couldn't see Deborah's red Mazda MX5 parked anywhere.

The governors had reluctantly agreed to Deborah's request for the Saturday detention but were pleased nonetheless that the large equipment shed was finally getting the sort-out that had been a long time coming. It was the former school assembly hall back in the sixties and had been used to store all of the school's tables, chairs, sports equipment, furniture and the like for the past forty years. There was decades of accumulated clutter, dirt, dust and god knew what else, probably rodents the size of dogs and winged creatures that breathed fire for all anyone knew.

That made Pamela laugh to herself as she locked her car door and walked toward the swimming pool, a couple of hundred feet away from the car-park. The equipment shed was hidden behind the pool, accessed by an overgrown, forgotten path that led around the outside, adjacent to the regularly used , wider path that led to the sports field nearby.

The pool was eerily quiet and deserted as Pamela walked toward the overgrown path, she looked in and as always found a still water unnervingly peculiar, there was always something quite sinister about a deserted pool that made the hair on the back of her neck stand to attention.

She wasn't a great lover of the water.

As she rounded the outside of the building, she thought she could hear laughter coming from up around the end of the pool building and she stopped where she stood, straining to hear after her footfalls fell silent.

There was nothing.

She then realised that there were no sounds at all; no wind in the tall trees that surrounded the pool building, no birds twittering in said trees, no sounds of children running around in the nearby play areas.

It was if the school had been placed inside a dome and was cut off from the world outside.

She cursed Stephen fricking King and his vivid, horrifying imagination.

And hers.

Pamela continued along the side of the building, brushing the over-hanging branches away from her face, her pumps-style deck shoes barely making a sound on the cracked asphalt as she rounded the back corner of the building.

There, basked in shafts of glistening sunlight in that chilly October morning, stood the ramshackle, wooden equipment shed, it's moss-covered outer shell dark against the sports fields that it stood alongside. The darkened windows were all open, yet offered no visibility as to what was inside, light unable to penetrate the gloom within. Outside the building, scores of chairs and old desks had been piled up around the entrance, bags of rubbish, old footballs and gym equipment seemingly thrown around like a maze outside the open double doors.

Then, as she was walking toward the monolithic stacks around the building, she heard laughter once again.

It sounded like a woman's laughter.

Pamela lowered her head, puffed out her cheeks and strode purposefully toward the building, skirting around the piles of furniture, striding confidently toward the sound of the laughter, determination to find out what the hell was going on, etched upon her face.

Her heart leapt into her throat as she came upon the open double-doors, a gasp escaping her open mouth as her jaw dropped.

Deborah Sheldon stood at the far end of the gloomy room, bathed in shafts of sunlight that cascaded down from the skylight above, her arms outstretched, her head thrown back in ecstasy.

Naked as a newborn.

The five boys, knelt around her in a semi-circle, five feet away, also naked, their twisted bodies writhing where they knelt, moans and laughter filling the room to the rafters.

Pamela could seen white tendrils of what resembled smoke, emanating from the boys, drawn to Deborah like moths to a flame, searching for her, snaking toward her outstretched fingers.

Deborah Sheldon was levitating two feet off the wooden floor.

Glowing brilliant white from head to toe, her once cropped black hair cascading down past her feet, squirming, writhing like snakes.

Then Deborah's head fell forward to reveal that her eyes were pure black, cold as night, deep as the lowest ocean.

And seemingly staring through Pamela, chilling her through to the bone, as if Deborah was staring deep into her very soul.

A clicking, screech came from Deborah's opening mouth and the five boys all turned their heads to look at Pamela, their eyes also as black as coal.

"Get her!" Deborah screamed, an unearthly guttural scream that cut like a razor blade through Pamela's skull.

And the boys were upon her, their cold, claw-like fingers digging into the soft flesh of her arms, hands over her mouth smothering any sound from her. She tried to pull herself free but was frogmarched into the surprisingly hot room, feet off the ground as she was propelled toward Deborah, who by this time, had floated back down to the floor.

"Stupid woman," Deborah hissed, "you should have stayed away from my feasting."

Pamela's eyes widened in shock and terror as Deborah's hair, alive and probing, shot out and snaked around Pamela's throat.

Pamela tried to scream as she was lifted off the ground, the hair tightening around her throat before enveloping her face, covering her head with wriggling tendrils, invading her open mouth.

The five boys giggled like infants as their little headmistress was devoured by their succubus's flaxen hair, covering her from head to toe until only her form remained.

Deborah's naked body putatively glowed as Pamela's life-force flowed through her, her cries of ecstatic pleasure becoming louder and louder before her hair released

Pamela's withered, skeletal body which slumped to the floor at her feet.

"Not as powerfully sating as a young man's spirit," Deborah's voice screeched through the silence, "but that should tide me over for the time being."

The boys looked upon the body of Pamela and as Deborah pulled on her dark blue blouse and blue jeans, the five of them picked up the husk of their headmistress and carried it to the back of the room. Pushing aside the old wooden Vault-Horse, they exposed the opening in the floor that had been hidden for countless years.

The hole that bodies had been hidden down for hundreds of years.

The corpse of Pamela landed twenty-feet below upon the skeletal remains of some fifty men, women and children. Men, women and children that Deborah had sacrificed to her insatiable lust for life.

Since the 1800's, when she had first stumbled across this strange little town with its location upon very powerful Ley lines and it's paranormal phenomena, Deborah had emerged every twenty-five years or so to feast upon the life-spirit of it's inhabitants.

The teacher vacancy had been a literal god-send, she could get closer to the children like never before.

And gave her the perfect access to her old dumping round for the bodies of the poor lost souls.

As the boys moved toward her, their hands reaching for her lithe, supple body, Deborah laughed, feeling their fingers creeping along her torso, caressing her, kneading her soft skin.

The headmistress job was now vacant.

And she knew of the perfect candidate.

JUSTIN CHARLES MASON

THE WALL

The house stood at the corner of Main Street and Badley Street, one of Oakleigh's oldest buildings, built sometime in the 16th century, for the wealthy landowner, Thomas Richards. It was originally part of the large Manor House that overlooked the blossoming town all those many years ago and although many of the other buildings had disappeared or had been amalgamated into more modern and up-to-date dwellings, 25 Main Street was the last standing. Further up, the Bed & Breakfast, Highfields Lodge, had been built on the former site of the main house but Number 25 had the original foundations, inner walls, even original beams, incorporated in the fabric of the building. The original wainscoting panelling had been replaced back in the 1800's and was still there in the downstairs of the house, albeit painted brilliant white over the original riven oak.

And rarely for Oakleigh houses, it had a cellar.

The had been one of the reasons Oliver and Penny Williams had fallen in love with the place, that and the price which was an absolute steal in this current climate. The newly-weds both worked in the financial sector in nearby Taunton and were living with their affluent parents before their marriage a few weeks previously..They had received quite a sum from both sets of parents, enabling them to pay a hefty deposit that left them with a pittance of a monthly mortgage payment, which they easily could afford on their salaries.

They hadn't needed to decorate as the property, standing empty for a number of years, had been purchased by a local builder and decorator and put on the market for well below the asking price that would have been expected of such a property and they had literally bitten the hand of the pretty, blonde estate agent from Chard.

Moving day came around pretty quick, in early July, it was a gloriously sunny day when the furniture started to arrive from the local stores, everything brand new, expensive and bespoke. Oliver and Penny had both taken the day off and were sifting through the small boxes of private knick-knacks they had managed to transport across in their car. Parking had been a nightmare which was the only drawback with the house's location but they had managed to find somewhere at the very end of Bodley Street. Luckily, their personal belongings weren't too heavy.

Penny naturally, had made Oliver carry them.

She was now sat cross-legged upon the polished wooden floor in the lounge, sorting the framed pictures into two neat piles, one lot for the wall, one lot for the surface areas. she was wearing a loose sweatshirt over her black leggings. Oliver, in jeans and a Pink Floyd t-shirt, was busy re-arranging the large, L-shaped, purple sofa in the far corner of the room. He was struggling slightly as the removal men had just plonked it in the middle of the large room when they brought it in.

He cursed them under his breath, their heavy footfalls coming from upstairs as they carried the four-poster bed and oak bedroom furniture into the large bedroom, directly over their heads. At least they had put the huge display unit against the wall, it meant he wouldn't have to lump it around, so he was quite thankful for that.

Collapsing breathless upon the newly-aligned sofa, Oliver looked appreciatively at his new wife sitting amidst the chaos of the pictures and assorted decorative pieces. He could see the curve of her small breasts hanging against her loose sweatshirt and he smiled to himself at the thought of the two of them trying out their newly-purchased & newly-assembled bed being put together as they sat there. It had been a couple of weeks since the two of them had been intimate, their wedding night seemed so far back and they'd found it difficult to get any free time while staying with Penny's parents. Save for a quick grope and hurried blow-job which although rather nice, wasn't the same for Oliver.

He decided they would make up for lost time that very evening.

Penny wouldn't know what hit her.

That made his smile widen as he looked at her and when she raised her head to see him grinning like some loon as he sat on the sofa, Penny knew what the bugger was smiling about.

She was thinking it too.

They christened virtually every room that evening, indeed making up for lost time but Penny drew the line at the basement. There was nothing down there at the moment, Oliver's gym equipment wasn't being delivered for a few more days, so at the moment it was a bare, white room, with oak panelling like the rest of the downstairs. More importantly, there was no surface that they could utilise while making love.

Penny sat in the plush, purple armchair, wearing just one of Oliver's shirts, while he lay across the sofa, smoking a cigarette and looking at her. She was again cross-legged, breathless, trying desperately to catch her breath while listening to the Friday night revellers, outside in the town centre.

It was a little after 11pm.

"Quite an eventful day, dear," she sighed, a wry smile on her face, "let's hope married life isn't always this hectic!"

Oliver exhaled loudly, a plume of smoke rising to the high, exposed beams.

"This honeymoon period will last for quite a while yet, sweetheart." he laughed, winking suggestively at her.

"You'd best take me back upstairs and prove it will." Penny replied, letting her fingers snake down the front of her half-open shirt, raising and lowering her feint eyebrows in a passable impression of Groucho Marx.

Oliver awoke sometime later, hearing laughter.

Rolling over, he fumbled for his iPhone and saw it was a little after 3.30am. Penny was snoring softly beside him, her hair blonde ringlets tousled across her face as she lay on her side facing him.

He kissed her gently on the forehead and she murmured appreciatively in her sleep as he swung his legs out of the bed, clumping softly upon the carpeted floor. Oliver pulled on his boxer shorts and padded somewhat uneasily over to the large bay window, pulling the blind to one side.

The street below, where he assumed the laughter had come from, was deserted, bathed in the warm, yellow glow of the street-lights that lined Oakleigh's Main Street. He wondered if the people had moved into Bodley Street and craned his neck to see if he could see but was unsuccessful. Yawning, he walked slowly across to the hallway and looking out of the window there, he could see that Bodley Street was just as quiet, no one was there.

The laughter came again.

Oliver stood at the top of the stairs, peering down into the gloom of the darkened hallway and downstairs, convinced that the laughter had come from inside the house.

His heart raced, the hairs on the nape of his neck prickled and he felt his balls tightening.

The laughter wasn't discernable male or female, it was too short in brevity for him to differentiate between the two.

He flicked on the lights that flooded the landing and the hallway beneath him, making him blink at the ferocity of the light.

There was nothing there.

He was sure he'd locked both the front and back doors before they had ascended for round two of frantic love-making and strained his mind to remember if he was sure he had.

Despite his state of undress, he walked slowly and quietly down the stairs, expecting a creaking step to give him away at any second, holding his breath for what seemed like an eternity. He stood in the hallway, listening out for any sound between the kitchen and the lounge, seemingly only hearing his heartbeat as he debated which door to go through.

He wished he knew where the actual light-switches were. He didn't relish the prospect of reaching through the dark, having to grope for them, dreading a cold, clammy hand to fall on his arm and pull him in. The little light that the hallway offered inside both rooms wasn't comforting in the slightest.

Steeling his resolve, he stepped quickly into the lounge, fumbling for the light-switch as his heart leapt into his mouth. Luckily, he found it instantly.

The room was empty.

Letting out an audible sigh of relief, he turned to look at the slightly ajar, kitchen door, gulping loudly and rushed toward it, flinging it open as he switched on the light.

It was empty also.

The back door, which led out into the walled courtyard, was firmly shut and as he rattled the door handle to confirm it was locked, he peered into the darkness outside. He couldn't see a thing in the gloom. And decided that tomorrow he would be getting alarms fitted and a motion-sensor light for the back door.

Walking back into the hallway, Oliver switched off the lounge and kitchen lights and walked slowly back up the stairs.

As he lay down next to the still sleeping Penny, he wrapped his arm around her shoulders and nuzzled his face into her neck. She moaned softly but didn't awaken.

It took Oliver about half an hour to finally get off back to sleep.

He'd realised that he hadn't checked the cellar.

Oliver and Penny's first week in the new house had positively flown by and the weekend following, they had thrown a little house-warming party, for their parents and their closest friends. It was a pretty low-key but entertaining night but Penny had wished her good friend Layla had been able to make it. She'd gone away for a few weeks, some seminar up country or something and Penny missed her terribly, she was definitely the life and soul of the party. Oliver himself was disappointed that she hadn't been there, she was a fire-cracker and rather hot to say the least. Not that he had such thoughts these days of course, he was a married man he told himself. Didn't stop him looking though.

Emma and Martin, Penny's parents and Harry and Wendy, Oliver's parents were the last ones at the end of the evening, all the others had decided to go into the town and finish their revelry in The Hangman's Arms public house, something that hadn't appealed to Penny and Oliver.

Penny, her mother and her mother-in-law were clearing up the kitchen while the men had gone downstairs, into the cellar, to check out Oliver's new gym equipment.

The three women stood chatting at the kitchen sink,

THE WALL

Wendy stood with a very large glass of red, looking slightly worse for wear as Penny washed and Emma wiped. All three of them were laughing and joking.

Wendy, her understated, yet elegant black cocktail dress seeming to look less and less than refined as she slouched against the sink, put the glass to her lips and managed to drop the entire contents down her front. She cried out in embarrassed surprise, exclaiming loudly what a dumb bitch she was.

Penny and her mother laughed louder at that.

"Mum, I'll take Wendy upstairs to get cleaned up."

Emma nodded, stifling her laughter as best she could, holding the dish-cloth to her chest as she leant against the sink herself.

She heard her daughter lead Wendy upstairs and turned to continue with the large amount of drying she had been left with.

Without warning, Emma could feel hot breath on the nape of her neck and a pair of hands snake around her torso, cupping her breasts through the satin of her red blouse. She let out an audible gasp and threw back her head moaning as she felt fingers probing for her nipples and hard lips upon her neck.

"Martin," she laughed in protest, "this is hardly the time or the place. Can't you wait until we get home?"

She opened her eyes as she turned.

She let out a loud gasp.

She was alone.

Fear crackled up her spine as she dropped the plate she had been drying, her scream fighting against the bile rising in her throat as she felt her drink coming back up. She fell backward, collapsing against the kitchen unit, feeling the world swimming before her eyes, as she looked down at her beige slacks.

She'd wet herself.

Oliver, his father and father-in-law emerged in the doorway of the kitchen, the three of them open-mouthed at the sight of Emma cowering and shivering in the middle of the kitchen, standing in a puddle of what looked very much like piss.

"What the hell, Emma?" Martin exclaimed, partly out of wonder and partly out of embarrassment, "have you fucking pissed yourself?"

Emma's mouth opened wordlessly, her green eyes looking imploringly at her rapidly angering husband who walked over to her and roughly grabbed her by the wrist.

"Ollie, tell our Penny that I'm taking her lush of a mother home."

Emma started to protest as the dish-cloth fell to the floor but Martin pulled her unceremoniously out of the kitchen, threw her coat at her and bundled her out of the front door before anyone could say a word, his hand roughly guiding her by what looked like a fistful of her hair.

"What the hell is happening?" Penny said quizzically as she walked back downstairs, quickly followed by Wendy who was wearing one of Penny's sweatshirts and tracksuit-bottoms.

"Wendy, we'd better be leaving too." Harry sighed, looking somewhat embarrassed himself but no one could tell if it was because of what had just happened with Emma & Martin or the inebriated state of his own wife.

Oliver and Penny were left open-mouthed in the kitchen, looking at each other as if to ask 'what the fuck?'

Oliver told Penny to go on up, he'd finish off the clearing up, she protested but he was insistent so she sighed, kissed him on the cheek and told him not to be long.

Slipping off her white and black wrap-around dress at the foot of the four-poster bed, Penny felt a sudden chill in the air and wrapped her arms around her underwear-clad body, shivering as she reached for her silk gown draped over the bedroom chair.

She then noticed that the heavy, Victorian-style

curtains were pulled around the bed.

And her heart leapt into her mouth as she heard the bed creak.

Tying the belt of her robe too tight around her slender waist, she gulped loudly and pulled back the heavy drape.

The bed was empty.

Cursing loudly, she left out a gasp of relief and reached inside her robe, deftly removing her white bra and stepping out of her white knickers, kicking them toward the bedroom chair against the far wall.

She shivered again as the cold chill descended once again and throwing back the silk sheets, jumped unceremoniously into the bed, grumbling loudly at the cold, reminding herself that she'd get Oliver to look at the heating tomorrow and get the duvet out of the cupboard.

Not long after, she heard the curtain around the bed open and felt Oliver slide into bed beside her, feeling his cold arms slide around her, an equally cold hand sliding inside the opening of her robe. She smiled to herself, eyes closed as his fingers tweaked her nipple to erection and she moaned softly. She let out a playful groan as she felt his other hand lift the hem of her robe and almost let out a cry of pleasure as he entered her from behind, his hot breath in her ear, his fingers pulling harder on her nipple.

He started thrusting into her hard, her cries of pleasure becoming louder then she felt him grab a handful of her short, black hair and turning her face into the luxurious pillow, he forced her onto her front. She tried to protest as he roughly shoved her face into the pillow and rammed himself into her, catching her breath as he relentless powered into her. Penny struggled to breathe, her hand reaching up to claw at his hand on the back of her head as he pressed her head down harder.

Her nails scraped at what felt like a coarse, leather glove upon his hand.

Then he suddenly stopped and his entire weight

slipped off of her.

Penny furiously spun over, ready to give him a piece of her mind, extremely annoyed that he could use her like a whore, scare her with holding her face-down.

She was alone in the bed.

Oliver heard Penny scream as he was at the foot of the stairs just about to venture up to bed. He ran up the straight staircase, taking two steps at a time, his heart beating like an express train in his constricting chest.

As he reached the bedroom doorway, he caught sight of Penny sat bolt upright in bed, the robe held together at her chest threatening to slip off her bare shoulders, tears in her eyes, her body racking with silent sobs.

"What is it?" Oliver gasped, sitting next to her on her side of the bed, his arms reaching for her.

Penny flinched at his touch, pulling her robe tighter together, moving away from him like he was some diseased leper who touch would contaminate her.

She stared at him, fear and despair in her beautiful blue eyes.

She never said a word.

Oliver tried in vain to get her to tell him what happened and after nearly an hour of pleading and begging, he felt a twinge of anger rise, throwing his hands up in the air with exasperation and frustration.

He started to get up and leave the room when she finally spoke.

Just three words. Quietly and barely above a whisper.

"Don't leave me."

The following morning, Penny wouldn't leave Oliver's side yet still wouldn't offer an explanation as to what had made her scream last night or why she looked drained, scared and didn't want to be left alone.

She looked visibly relieved when he suggested they take a drive out to the coast and positively skipped out of the front door in jeans, heavy jumper, silk scarf and winter coat, her hair scraped back, a baseball cap pulled down over her eyes.

Yet she still wouldn't tell him about last night.

When they returned, she stood at the front door and told him she was going to see her parents.

Oliver tried to say that he'd go with her but she shot him down in flames before the words even left his mouth, kissing him on the cheek and making her way down Bodley Street where she'd parked her Golf Gti.

Oliver went inside, shutting the large front door and kicking off his walking boots, slipping off his coat, he decided to go down to the cellar and work off his bewilderment at Penny's behaviour.

Stripping down to his t-shirt and tracksuit bottoms, he placed his iPhone in the Bluetooth cradle and started his Linkin Park playlist, "Papercut" filling the room to the rafters, the oak panelling shaking as the bass kicked in.

Oliver sat in the rowing machine and pulled himself backwards and forwards in time with the music, oblivious to the vigorous shaking of the panelling directly behind him. It started to bow, backwards and forwards in time with his exertions on the rowing machine, as if a breathing monster was behind it. It started to crack at the bottom, coming away from the brickwork behind it.

Oliver felt the air chill around him, the goosebumps rising upon his sweat-covered arms and he shivered involuntarily, watching his breath form clouds of silvery haze as he breathed in and out.

The wall behind him seemed to pulsate, the brickwork behind crumbling, a few of the bricks working their way loose.

Oliver heard something behind him and turning his head, he saw the strip of wooden panelling fall forward, crashing to the floor beside him.

He cursed loudly, standing up from the rowing machine, aiming to give those cowboy builders a piece of his mind as soon as he'd investigated further. If there was one thing he couldn't stand, it was shoddy workmanship and being ripped off, even if the house had been a complete steal, it was no goddamn excuse.

Wiping the sweat from his eyes with his equally wet arm, he walked toward the broken panelling, feeling a cool draft around his ankles where the bricks had fallen loose, the smell of hundreds of years of damp decay, nauseatingly strong in his nostrils.

It smelt as if something had died in that cellar.

Oliver picked up the panelling that had fallen to the ground and leant it against the wall opposite, surveying the brickwork that had been exposed. He thought that the wall should have been a load-bearing wall that skirted the foundations but it suddenly dawned on him that there was space behind, as if there was another chamber further under the house. He could feel a faint hum coming from the exposed bricks and carefully placed his outstretched hand upon them.

The humming stopped as abruptly as it had started.

Oliver's head started to ache something fierce and he blinked away the pain, walking back up the stairs to his toolbox in the hallway cupboard, under the stairs.

He found his big, bulky torch and made his way back down to the cellar. As he descended the wooden stairs, his headache almost made him stumble and he had to steady himself against the cool wall, closing his eyes tightly.

He never heard the laughter coming from the cellar, deep, foreboding and unmistakably male.

As he stepped back in to the brightly-lit cellar, his arms started to feel extremely heavy and the torch nearly fell from his grasp but he steadied himself and walked toward the opening in the bricks. He could feel nausea and unconsciousness pulling at him as he sank to his knees and put his face toward the hole, the torch beside his heavy head. Placing his spare hand against the brick to steady himself, he was about to peer inside when the bricks gave way and he tumbled head first into the bigger hole he had just created, his stomach falling heavily on the bottom edge.

Oliver cried out involuntarily as he felt the bricks scrape his stomach and as he let go of the torch, it skidded across dust-covered floor, crashing loudly against the far wall of the enclosed space. It had stopped about four feet away.

He pulled himself up onto his elbows and stared into the semi-gloom of the space beyond, squinting against the darkness, barely illuminated by the fallen torch.

It looked like there was a small ante-chamber attached to the cellar, no more than four foot squared, bare, covered in a thick layer of dust.

Except for the skeleton sat against the far wall, its skull hanging down as if on its chest, its sallow bones covered in what looked like pieces of dirty rags, obviously clothing that the body had been left in.

What chilled Oliver to the bone was the skeleton's hand reaching out toward him, it's bony fingers seemingly bidding him to come closer.

Groaning slightly, he pulled himself through the widened hole and clambered slowly to his feet, brushing off the dust and cobwebs that covered his chest, his hair as he crouched slightly.

There was barely room enough to stand.

Linkin Park continued to play behind him, "Somewhere I Belong" starting to kick in.

Oliver thought that what he was currently stood, with his head lowered, was possibly a priest-hole, a left over from the mid 16th century but being a bit of a history geek, he knew that this house was dated from the mid 17th century, so was more than a little confused.

And the gnawing dull ache in his head had started to get worse, he shook it to try and clear his thoughts but to no avail.

The spectre of the skeleton loomed large in the semi-darkness and retrieving the torch from where it had fallen, he brought it to bear upon it, marvelling how clean the bones were. He expected more decayed skin, more 'gunk', something more akin to the 'Walkers' in that American t.v rubbish, 'The Walking Dead'.

His head pounded more and more violently, making his teeth chatter in his open mouth, which he slammed shut, crying out in pain.

The music had fallen quiet behind him, the silence becoming almost unbearable as his head threatened to explode, he thrust his fists against his temple but to no avail.

As Oliver's eyes flicked open, he thought for a brief moment that the eye-sockets of the skeleton's skull had glowed faintly a reddish orange, despite the light of the torch being brilliant white upon the ivory bones.

Then the ache that blinded him in its ferocity, abruptly stopped.

As a soft, deep voice spoke.

"That woman is a harlot."

Oliver blinked incredulously.

It sounded like the voice was in his head, sounded like it was from all around him, sounded like it came from the bones before him.

"She fornicates with others," the voice hissed, "and she enjoys the sins of the flesh."

Oliver stumbled backwards, knocking his head against the opening of the brickwork behind him, dust falling in his hair and in his face.

The voice, though soft and deep, sounded almost slithery, almost leathery, as if there were too many teeth in the mouth from whence it came. And there was an underlying hint of malice in it's words.

The ache in his head may have dissipated but Oliver's body was no racked with cramps that seemed to emanate from his very bones and he had to steady himself against the wall behind as he started to feel as if he was losing his balance, threatening to fall into the bones that sat before him.

"And the harlot must be punished," the voice continued, this time seemingly coming from within inches of his ear and he could almost feel hot breath, "and the punishment is death."

"She's my wife and I love her!" Oliver protested, his voice echoing in the small chamber, his lip trembling as much as his cramping body.

"Which is why YOU must be the one to punish her. The harlot must die."

Penny parked the car at the end of Bodley Street, where she did most days but sat there for a good half an hour before exiting the vehicle, her baseball cap pulled down over her eyes. The unscheduled trip to see her parents had been a ruse but it had turned out to be a rather educational and particularly eye-opening visit.

She had found out that her father had rather viscously slapped her mother the previous night, leaving a bruise below her right eye, apparently the first time he had ever struck her in nearly thirty years of marriage. Penny had slapped him that afternoon, screaming that his first time had better have been the last. Martin had burst into tears, shame and embarrassment pricking his conscience as he cowered in their large, open-plan kitchen, Emma crying into her hands while sitting at the breakfast bar. Emma had apparently told Martin that Oliver and Penny's house was haunted, that there was a malevolent force there and he'd blamed the copious amount of alcohol she'd necked like there was no tomorrow.

Penny had stared open-mouthed as her father recounted her mother's words at what she'd experienced in Penny's kitchen, felt the bile rise in the back of her throat, her parent's kitchen swimming before her very eyes.

The memories of the previous night had of course been at the forefront of her mind all day despite trying to bury them deep and they flooded back with such vivid clarity that she could feel the hand buried deep in her hair, the taste of the cotton pillow filling her mouth, her nostrils.

Penny had thrown up upon her parent's kitchen floor before sinking to her knees, sobbing her heart out.

The ten minute drive from Chard seemed to take an eternity, Penny's entire body sheathed in a fine layer of perspiration, despite the chattering of her teeth and her inability to find warmth, even though her winter coat was buttoned up and the car heaters on full.

And now here she was, contemplating not even going home to her new home, sitting in her boiling hot car, watching the townsfolk walk past her house, oblivious to the apparent evil that may have dwelt within.

Penny locked her Golf as she slammed the car door, pulling down her baseball cap tighter, pulling up the collar of her coat, an imaginary wind seemingly whistling around her.

The sun shone brightly overhead, the late summer blue sky laced with silvery clouds that cast long shadows, as she stepped toward home, a creeping malaise rising up from the small of her back.

Her heart threatened to burst out of her chest.

Turning the key in the front-door's lock, she tentatively stepped over the threshold.

The house was as silent as a graveyard.

Penny called out for Oliver and heard him call out from the cellar, his voice slightly muffled as if he was far away, even possibly like he was underwater.

He shouted for her to come on down.

Penny slipped off her hat and coat, hanging them on the coat-hooks just inside the front door, dropping her keys in the bowl on the small table against the wall, rubbing her cold arms as if the cold would never leave her.

Her walking boots clumped noisily upon the wooden floorboards and as she approached the staircase that led down to the cellar, she heard Oliver's footsteps coming up toward her.

He popped suddenly into view, his half-naked body covered in sweat and looked to Penny as dust and dirt.

Oliver was grinning.

"You'll never believe what I've found down here!" he claimed excitedly, "come and have a look!"

He took her hand and Penny involuntarily shivered at how clammy and cold it was, his fingers as cold as the icicles that seemed to be dancing up her spine.

She resisted the urge to scream as he dragged her down the stairs, coming face to face with a huge hole in the far wall of the cellar, darkness looming inside, dark and oppressive, looking for all the world like an open maw.

And there sat upon the floor, outside the hole, was a complete skeleton.

"What the fuck?" Penny exclaimed, her dismay visible upon her face that was draining of all colour, a throbbing ache exploding behind her eyes.

Oliver looked up at her, his grin not dissipating as he knelt before the skeleton, his bare torso shimmering beneath the fluorescent light from above, his muscles seemingly stretching like a coiled spring.

"This is Brandir Carver," Oliver laughed, as if he was introducing an old friend, "he was hiding from Judge Jeffrey's persecution after the Monmouth rebellion."

Penny stood at the foot of the stairs, her mouth staying open, her silk scarf suddenly feeling as constricting as a noose even though it was laying loose around her neck.

"How the fuck do you know that, Ollie?" she stammered.

His grin quickly faded.

"He told me." he stated coldly, his words hanging in the air, almost as if waiting for her to question him.

Penny started to say something but he grabbed her by both arms, his strong hands, grasping her through the soft wool of her heavy jumper, in a vice-like grip that made her cry out in pain and alarm.

"He also told me about you fucking other men." he growled menacingly, his finger nails digging into her slender arms, "told me you are a whore."

Penny tried to protest but the words wouldn't come as cold tendrils of fear shot up from the pit of her stomach, Oliver's clear blue eyes seemingly staring right through her, boring through hers with an intensity that almost stopped her heart.

She then watched in fear and panic as Oliver grabbed the ends of her silk scarf and stumbling backwards she felt the wall cold against her back, his eyes still upon her.

As he pulled the scarf tightly around her throat, she could hear soft, menacing chuckling begin to fill the cellar, knowing damn well that it wasn't coming from Oliver.

It seemed to fill the cellar to it's exposed beams, filling the entire house from foundations to the roof, the resonating sound enveloping her as the darkness pulled at her where she stood.

Oliver stood beneath the warm jets of the shower, a small wry smile on his face as he washed away the dirt and grime, whistling an unknown hymn that seemed vaguely familiar but name escaped him at that time.

The skeleton was back behind the wall, the bricks put back, the wall re-plastered, the wainscoting put back in place more securely this time. Oliver would complain to the builder given the chance but thought it was probably for the best to let sleeping dogs lie for now.

And his wife also.

Oliver washed himself clean, still whistling.

It was Morning Hymn, written by Rev Thomas Ken in 1674:

THE WALL

Awake, my soul, and with the sun thy daily stage of duty shake off dull sloth, and early rise to pay thy morning sacrifice

JUSTIN CHARLES MASON

MEMORIES FADE

The young man, probably no more than thirty-five at the most, looked up from the bed where he lay and stared blankly at the man and woman stood before him. He looked from the tall brunette woman, to the short, bald man, both dressed in identical white, knee-length coats and his brown eyes bore into them.

He had no idea who they were.

The tall woman, named Vanessa Mansfield and the short man, named Victor Quentin were both doctors, Victor, a neurological consultant, Vanessa, a psychiatrist, both called in by the locum Dr. Hilary Winkler, Oakleigh General Hospital's resident physician.

They had been called in after the man had returned from Musgrove park Hospital in Taunton, earlier that morning,after he had been sent there for a CT scan and MRI.

There seemed to be no neurological or physical trauma that could explain why this man, found wandering Oakleigh Main Street, covered in blood, could not remember anything. Not his name, where he came from or indeed, who's blood he was covered from head to toe with.

The local constabulary had scoured the entire town and surrounding areas but there seemed to be no trace of anyone, or anything that could explain the blood found on the young man. Frank Lewis, Oakleigh's police sergeant had questioned the man extensively and had become frustrated at the lack of information, so had posted WPC Olivia Cole outside his door, for the foreseeable future.

To make sure nothing further happened to the young man.

And more importantly, he didn't make a run for it.

His picture and his fingerprints had been taken but nothing had turned up from the National Crime Database and although the man was coherent and had spoke nothing but English, his details had been sent to Interpol. On the off-chance he was actually a foreign national.

His Somerset accent, quite a strong one at that, had made that more than a bit moot but Frank believed in being thorough. And anything that cropped up would help no end.

Unlike nearby Chard, which cried out for CCTV in the town centre due to raucous Friday and Saturday shenanigans from the pissed and the 'high' idiots that lived there, Oakleigh was quiet enough not to warrant such measures. Which Frank thought was a shame but secretly was quite glad that wasn't the case.

But in this instance, it may have been able to shed some light onto where this man had come from.

Vanessa approached the hospital bed and perched precariously on the edge as she started to speak to the young man, her pretty green eyes on his as she smiled warmly.

The two of them looked intently into each other's eyes and Vanessa felt some sort of connectivity between them, feeling a hot flush upon her chest, the collar of her light blue, buttoned shirt suddenly feeling rather tight and constricting, although the top two buttons were undone.

The man was unnaturally handsome, with chiselled

features, a strong jaw, shoulder-length brown hair and mesmerizing, deep, brown eyes. His muscular torso and thick neck seemed two sizes too small for the t-shirt he was wearing, the locally-purchased pyjama set, with black shorts, had been hastily purchased when the clothes he had been wearing had been sent away for forensics to pour over.

He was a thick set man with the biggest hands Vanessa had ever seen and although he exuded power and sheer, brute strength, his eyes were warm and inviting enough to make her go a little weak at the knees. She desperately fought the urge to start unbuttoning her shirt and throw herself upon him with wanton abandonment.

But only just.

Victor watched his colleague lean toward the young man and though for a moment that she was going to reach out and caress his face, watching her small, yet pert chest strain against the cotton of her shirt. He could feel his mouth start to gape open and slammed it shut with such force that his teeth clattered nosily together, making him jump and almost cry out in alarm.

Vanessa and the man looked up at him and he smiled, hoping to God that it wasn't as loud as it had sounded in his head.

"We have been unable to find anything physically wrong with you," Vanessa started, a strand of her brown hair falling down over her eye, which she brushed away from her face, "so we are surmising that it may be something psychological. I therefore have suggested that we continue with some intensive sessions over the coming days."

The man nodded, not saying a word , his eyes darting between Vanessa and Victor once more.

Frank Lewis walked through the entrance to the hospital, lowering his head slightly as not to bang his head upon the metal frame. At 6' 7" tall and well over twenty stone, his imposing frame just about managed to get through the door and striding purposely to the reception area, he caught sight of the blonde, Ward Sister, chatting nonchalantly to the petite receptionist.

He'd always had a soft spot for Jennifer Goodwin, the tall, matronly woman that presided over the small hospital, reminding him of a statuesque prison warden in some sleazy, sexploitation movie from the 1970's. Curvy and flirtatious, with a pair of tits that Frank would die for, she wore that blue tunic conservatively, though Frank often wished that he could get hold of that zipper at the front to give her a deeper cleavage.

This made him smile as he approached her and as if she'd read his mind, she thrust that rather large chest in his direction as she smiled warmly at him, a cliched, mischievous glint in her blue eyes.

"Sgt. Lewis, a pleasure as always!" she said loudly, leaning on her hands on the edge of the reception desk.

"Likewise, Sister Goodwin," he retorted with that broad grin of his, "I understand the man has returned from Taunton?"

Sister Goodwin nodded, her chest jiggling as she did so, Frank adamant that she was doing it on purpose.

"Would you like me to take you?"

Frank thought of a rather dirty response but decide to keep it to himself.

It contained the phrase 'back-passage'.

"That would be very kind of you, Sister." Frank replied, watching her slide effortlessly around the desk and lead him toward the lift doors, at the end of the short, sparse corridor.

Inside the lift, Frank resisted the strong urge to glance down the front of her tunic and mercifully, the short trip between floors took barely an instant.

He knew that she'd be powerless to stop him if he acted upon his lecherous thoughts.

But he would have hoped she would have least put

up some kind of fight.

Stepping into the upper corridor, Frank caught sight of his WPC sat outside the private room, her nose buried in some trashy, horror novel and he tutted beneath his breath. The Ward Sister smiled up at him, her eyes lingering upon his face as he smiled back at her, thanking her for the accompaniment to the room.

"Anytime, Sergeant." Sister Goodwin said softly.

Frank thought he'd probably hold her to that.

Coughing to signal his arrival, WPC Cole almost leapt from her chair, her paperback falling nosily at her feet, loud upon the clean, sterile floor. She placed her hand upon her chest to signal that her heart was pounding like a jack-hammer, taking a theatrical deep breath.

Frank tried not to smile.

"Keeping busy?" he growled, towering over her, his imposing size almost dwarfing her.

She looked up at him, bending to pick up her paperback which she sheepishly placed back upon the plastic chair she had been sitting on.

"The patient has a couple of doctors with him, sir," Olivia replied stiffly, her blue eyes cast downwards as looking at her Sergeant gave her such a crick in the neck, "there's nothing much happening."

Frank studied his charges' petite yet curvy frame, her plain, unremarkable features, her cropped, streaked blonde pulled back in a small, loose ponytail and wished she looked a little prettier. It would make it harder to bollock her off if she stirred something in his loins.

Unluckily for her, Sister Goodwin had given him a warm glow and in all honesty, a more than hot crotch, so he'd let WPC Cole's lackadaisical demeanour slide.

For now.

The door to the private room opened and a tall woman and short man emerged, Frank's eyes typically drawn to the leggy brunette who was replacing her glasses on her face as she walked through.

"I'm Sgt. Lewis," Frank stated authoritatively, thrusting his open hand toward the woman that bypassed the man with almost savage precision and almost knocked him to one side, "anything to report?"

Vanessa shook the sergeant's hand, impressed with his firm grip and yet softness of his hand, sniggering inwardly that he'd made a bee-line for her rather than Victor, who was closer.

"My colleague and I have ruled out certain kinds of amnesia due to the lack of evident physical trauma, so we are considering dissociative amnesia." Vanessa said, her eyes upon the cold eyes of the policeman.

"Can he be treated?" Olivia asked, immediately shut down by a withering look from Frank, that almost screamed that she should shut up and let the adults speak.

She shut up straight away.

"The blood found upon him has been identified as that of an adult male but we need to know where the hell it has come from," Frank sighed, "finding out who this weirdo is, is the least of my worries to be honest."

The man looked at the congregated group through the hospital door and somehow knew that the tall policeman, despite his uniform and amiable behaviour, was not to be trusted. He didn't know how, but he also knew that the female doctor wanted him, the male doctor wanted the female doctor and the WPC that had been sat outside his door, wanted her superior.

He could tell all this with just a look but for the life of him, couldn't know who the hell he was, where the hell he was from or why the hell he had come to this pissant, crummy little town.

Being found drenched in someone else's blood, with no memory and an insatiable, unquenchable thirst for truth was all that he did know at that present time.

He sat there, turning his attention back to the white wall, and tried, in vain, to search every corner of his mind, struggling to remember more than the past hour. The female doctor, Vanessa, had told him about the blood, about being found wandering, he couldn't remember anything and couldn't hold any information in.

Not that he'd told her that. Nor would any time soon.

For the time being, if his fuddled mind let him of course, anything he did think or feel would be kept under wraps.

Yet he wasn't sure why.

And there was am underlying feeling, somewhere deep within the recesses of his scrambled thoughts, digging like some burrowing animal, that he needed to get out of this hospital.

He felt the people move away from the door outside and looked back to see the WPC sitting back down in her chair, the three others disappeared from view.

The woman guarding him would be easy to get past, she was too intent on reading that trashy horror novel to notice if he was to slip out of the door, he knew he could render her unconscious if need be.

Somehow he knew that he could twist her head clean off her shoulders if he wanted to and that initial thought scared him more than a little.

But excited him more.

The moon, as bright as the sun had been earlier in the day, hung in the cold night sky and illuminated the car park as Vanessa and Victor walked quickly and quietly toward where her car was parked. The policeman had walked in the opposite direction when exiting the small hospital, which instantly put Vanessa at ease. The was definitely something disconcerting about that giant of a man, the way he undressed her with his eyes, the way he intimidated her as he towered over her at every given opportunity. He scared her much more than the reported 'lunatic', currently sat upstairs in that hospital room without a name or any idea where he came from.

Blood or no blood, he didn't scare her halfway as much as Sgt. Frank Lewis.

Despite the warmth of the night air, she felt a shiver of trepidation slither up her spine at the thought of him.

Victor, deep in thought about his statuesque colleague, didn't see the figure emerge from the shadows and never knew what happened as the blade slid effortlessly between his fifth and sixth vertebrae, severing his spinal cord. He attempted to cry out but in one swift movement, the knife was at his throat, slitting from ear to ear.

Vanessa turned to see Victor collapsing upon the tarmac and with a scream lodged in her gullet, she saw the dark figure lurch swiftly toward her.

"Where is he?" the guttural voice hissed as a gloved hand encircled her throat, the cold blade pressing against her soft cheek, the point of the knife mere inches below her eye.

Victoria knew who this person meant without her heart skipping a beat.

She was pushed back against the nearest car, her legs threatening to buckle beneath her as the tip of the blade pierced her skin, a single droplet of blood trickling down her dampening cheek.

"Second floor," Vanessa stammered, "room 17B."

The hooded figure before her took the blade away and with one swift movement dropped the hood.

Vanessa came face to face with a black-haired, green-eyed woman of roughly the same height, same age and same look as the man currently residing in room 17B.

She assumed they were twins.

The woman standing before her stared impassively at her and with her gloved hand still on Vanessa's throat, thrust the blade into Vanessa's chest, to the hilt. Vanessa had no time to scream as her blood rose up from below, choking her off before she could make a sound.

Her lifeless body slumped to the ground, falling upon the prone corpse of her equally-dead colleague, the two of them in a final embrace, united in death more than they had ever been in life.

The dark-haired woman looked down at the two dead doctors and in the moonlight, her face started to melt, her pretty face beginning to resemble that of the more beautiful visage of dearly departed and even lovelier Vanessa. She dragged the two of them into the undergrowth with consummate ease, hiding their bodies out of sight.

She made no attempt to swap clothes with the woman whose face she now possessed. She believed there was no need.

The blackness of her hoody and leggings served a dual purpose and there seemed to be little reason to disregard the way they enabled her to melt into the shadows and made blood impossible to spot.

She put the switch-blade back into the hoodies' pocket and walked toward the hospital building.

Sister Goodwin looked up from the desk to see the delightful Vanessa re-enter the front door, smiling her best welcoming smile as she strode toward the desk. If she realised that Vanessa was now dressed all in black, she never made comment, she just rose from her seat and leant forward.

"Forget something Doctor?" she asked, her smile sincere yet somehow false.

Vanessa shook her head, not smiling, not saying a word.

"What happened to your partner?" she continued, moving slowly around the desk, her aching back creaking as she leant on the corner of the reception desk.

It had been a long shift.

Vanessa stopped alongside her and in one swift movement, Sister Goodwin felt white hot pain in her chest.

Looking down, she could see the hilt of what looked suspiciously like a knife, protruding from between her breasts.

She looked up at the eyes of Vanessa staring into hers and could see nothing there. They were dead eyes, reminding her in an instant as those of a shark, cold, dark and lifeless.

This was her last thought as the knife slid from her chest and was thrust upwards under her exposed chin.

She was dead before she slid to the linoleum floor at her feet, lifeless eyes closing for the final time.

The Vanessa woman dragged the dead Sister behind the desk and walked purposefully toward the stairs, wiping the bloody blade upon the hem of her top.

The man's eyelids flew open and he sat upright upon the bed, his neck muscles rigid and pronounced as he craned his head toward the door.

He knew someone was coming.

Images of dead bodies floated up from the recesses of his mind, the beautiful doctor and her short, rotund partner, the shapely, highly-sexed Ward Sister, the bloodied, lifeless corpses floating in some sort of tableau before his very eyes.

He shut then opened his eyes rapidly, as if trying to blink himself free of what he could see and he could imagine the door at the end of the corridor opening, the unsuspecting WPC unaware of the impending death and destruction heading her way.

He leapt from the bed, his bare feet slapping noisily upon the cold floor and in a flash, he was at the heavy fire-door, pulling it open and stepping into the light.

The policewoman went to get up from her chair, her novel falling to the floor but his hands were upon her shoulders before she could move. His hand went instinctively to the nape of her neck and as his fingers hit the pressure point behind her ear, she crumpled in his arms.

There wasn't time to try and understand how he knew how to render her unconscious and how easy it had been, he threw her over his shoulder and ran toward the fire exit at the end of the corridor, carrying her carefully, yet securely.

He heard the door at the opposite end of the corridor and as he pushed open the heavy fire-door, the alarm splitting the silence, he looked over his other shoulder.

Emerging from the staircase was a woman, dark-haired, dressed in black, an expression of calm, yet anger upon her familiar face.

The attractive ward sister was staring at him but he knew it wasn't really her, not just the hair colour failing to deceive him.

She was grinning an evil smile and as he stared open-mouthed at her, he could have sworn her face started to shimmer in the fluorescent light overhead, her features becoming tighter, her cheek-bones rising, her brow becoming more pronounced, her eyes changing from ice-blue to emerald-green.

It was suddenly a female version of his face.

He knew with from somewhere within his psyche, with apparent inherent aptitude that shocked and excited him in equal measure, that she wasn't a relative.

And that she was the threat he'd felt was coming for him.

He saw a blade being pulled from a pocket and saw her teeth bared as her lips revealed a vicious snarl, her eyes full of murderous intent.

He ran through the heavy door, carrying the unconscious policewoman, running down, taking three-steps at a time, the fire-door alarm still whining overhead. His bare feet slapped loudly upon the concrete of the stairs, yet he felt no pain, his legs absorbing every landing like coiled springs and projecting him down further.

He heard the door slam open above him and as he reached the bottom, he heard the woman above him, running hell for leather down the stairs in dogged pursuit. Emerging into the lobby of the hospital, he instantly saw the body of the deceased Ward Sister stuffed unceremoniously behind the reception desk, propped up against the wall in a pool of her own blood.

He made the instant decision to put the knocked-out policewoman behind the desk and in one swift movement, he threw her across the polished floor, her unconscious form sliding out of sight behind the nurse's body.

He turned as his pursuant crashed through the door and stood before him, knife in hand, her eyes upon him, a grin still plastered upon her face.

They stared at each other across the silent reception area like opposing gunslingers in some old black & white western, a look of confusion upon his face, a look of triumph upon hers.

The blade of the knife shined brightly as she twirled if deftly between her gloved fingers.

"Who are you?"

The woman sneered then laughed at him.

"You know." she hissed, "and you have to pay."

"For what? I don't remember anything!"

She threw back her head and laughed an exaggeratedly nefarious and somewhat staged laugh.

"For killing our father and escaping, you fucker!"

The words 'our father' hit him like the proverbial ton of bricks, a myriad of conflicting images suddenly flooding his mind as if something had opened the floodgates within his subconscious.

An image of a small, rodent-faced man in a long, white coat laying dead upon a cold, flag-stone floor in a widening pool of crimson blood, his throat ripped out. He was stood over him, his obscenely long fingers as sharp as razor-blades, positively dripping with the stuff before slowly shortening and becoming fingers once again. The room resembled a dungeon in some god-awful 1940's horror film, a single, metal framed bed in the middle of the room, chains and lichen covering the dank, damp walls, filthy water dripping from the wrought-iron ceiling.

The woman had been stood behind the man's body, chained to the wall and screaming obscenities, cursing him for killing their father, killing the man who made them who they were, created them.

Then images of torture, beatings, injections, shouting and abuse flooded his mind's eye, the pain, the agony, the abject humiliation coursing through his body.

He cried out and sank to his knees upon the floor in the reception, thrusting his fists against his temples, his eyes shut tightly as a scream erupted from deep within.

The woman flexed, coiled like a cobra about to strike, the blade held tightly in her hand, her grin fading as the man's eyes flicked open.

"You shouldn't have come for me," the man said, coldness in his deep voice resonating through the silence of the deserted hospital, "you should have let me disappear."

The woman growled, hate deep within her green eyes.

"I would kill every man, woman and child to get to you, you motherfucker, you killed the only man I ever loved."

"Let's cut the shit and just kill each other."

The woman leapt toward the man, her teeth bared once more, the blade slicing through the air, almost with a hiss. The woman's other hand morphed into a long, double-edged sword as she flew at the man, growling and spitting like a feral feline.

They came together with a deafening crash that sounded like metal on metal, their bodies entwining, the woman's two blades missing him as his hands found purchase upon her baggy clothes. They crashed to the floor, the woman frantically slashing at his face and torso but missing the mark as he ducked and weaved quicker than humanly possible.

Then he was on top of her, pinning her to the floor beneath his weight, her arms held down by his knees, his hands on her throat.

"You should have stayed away."

Her eyes widened in terror as his hands turned into blades above her.

He pulled them together without a second thought.

He looked down at her decapitated head after climbing off of her and kicking it to one side, he stepped away, looking down at her dead body, half expecting for her eyes to flick open, her arms and legs to move on their accord.

She didn't move.

Somewhere deep within the back of his mind, an idea leapt forward and without a moments hesitation he reached down and placed both hands, now resembling actual hands, upon her chest. His fingers started to glow as his eyes rolled up and the fallen woman laying before him started to glow the same unearthly green colour as his eyes.

Miraculously, the body started to become transparent before disappearing completely, the decapitated head with it, until nothing remained. No blood, now residue, no remnant of there ever being a body there at all.

His back cracked loudly as he stood back up, his eyes returning to their natural shade of light green, his face rippling then reverting to its rigid state as he walked to the body of the deceased Ward Sister. Her lifeless stared almost accusingly at him as he knelt beside her and placed his fingers upon her bloodied tunic.

His eyes started to glow, blue this time, electricity seemingly coursing from his fingers, directly into her knife wound.

Within seconds, her breasts started to rise and fall, breath catching in her throat as she blinked up at him, the blood reversing its flow, back into her body.

She cried out in shock and horror but couldn't utter a word.

He smiled down at her and put a finger to her lips.

"You wont remember a thing, Sister," he whispered softly, his flashing blue eyes seemingly boring into her, "within a few seconds, what has happened will seem like a nightmare you have woken from, you wont remember me either."

Sister Goodwin stared blankly at him, her mouth opening and closing like a fish producing bubbles and she closed her heavy eyelids as he picked her up and sat her back behind the desk, gently laying her head upon her folded arms upon the mahogany.

Vanessa's eyes flashed open, the breath catching in her throat as she sat bolt upright in the driver's seat of her Audi. Her hands were upon the steering wheel, the engine quietly idling as a local radio station told her it was 10pm. She looked across and Victor was sat next to her, his head back, snoring softly.

For the life of her, she couldn't remember where the hell she was and looking round, she caught sight of a blue sign.

She was sat in the car-park of Oakleigh Hospital.

She shook Victor awake, while still looking all around, to take in all of her surroundings and to see if anyone else was there.

"Victor!" she hissed, still vigorously shaking him from his deep slumber, "why the hell are we here?"

Victor, shaking his head to dislodge the remnants of his sleep, stammered and muttered, rapidly racking his brain as to why they had come to Oakleigh at this ungodly hour.

"I have no idea my dear," he stuttered, "simply no idea what so ever."

Victor felt a small, uncomfortable ache in the small of his back.

Vanessa felt a pain in her throat that felt like the first

tickle of an oncoming cold.

The two of them decided rather rapidly to drive back over to Taunton, the idea that they should get away from Oakleigh flooding their minds together and their discussion was extremely brief.

WPC Olivia Cole's eyes snapped open and she realised she'd fallen asleep in a plastic chair, while reading as it tipped and the book fell nosily to the floor as she fought to regain her balance. She let out a sigh of relief as he feet plonked safely upon the linoleum.

She then realised she had no idea why she was sat in this corridor. And more importantly, where the hell she actually was.

No matter how much she searched within her memory, there was no recollection of anything from the last 24 hours.

The only thing she did know was that Sgt. Lewis was probably going to chew her out YET again if she had to ask him what the hell was going on. He already thought she was an incompetent, blonde air-head and not knowing what had been happening for the last day would only confirm that for him.

She thought she ought to call-in.

But what the hell would she say?

The man walked upon the darkened street that cut through the town, his bare feet making no sound upon the pavement as he walked past the imposing edifice of the oldest building in Oakleigh, at the corner of Main Street and Bodley Street. The streets were devoid of traffic or even townsfolk, yet he still kept to the shadows between the pavement and the buildings and avoided the triangle of light near any street-lamp.

He knew he could have stolen any number of vehicle from the hospital car-park but he didn't want to alert anyone else to his presence within the local vicinity, either now, previously or in the future.

Snippets of memory had flooded back but not everything; he knew he could do a number of spectacularly amazing things that defied the laws of physics, human nature and belief in equal measure. He knew that the experiments and torture he had endured, had created him and condemned him just the same. He knew he was a killing machine with the capacity to heal and resurrect also. He knew that he could wipe a persons memory with just the power of his mind, even though his own mind was fractured.

He also knew that he had to get away from this town, others would come and hunt for him, others like him, others who possessed his abilities.

His clone had been the first of many that he believed would come his way, she had not been his equal but she had been lethal just the same.

And he knew that although he had killed 'Father', 'Mother' wouldn't let him get away.

'Mother' wouldn't let 'Father's' memory fade away either.

He carried on walking, deep into the warm night, fading into the darkness.

JUSTIN CHARLES MASON

HEAVEN OR HELL

The man and woman bought large lattes and sat at the very back of the Costa store. Despite the heat of the hot summer's day outside, they kept on their dark trenchcoats, at least, until they were seated. They were still wearing the obligatory black sunglasses but no one seemed to notice.

But as this was Chard, no one seemed to care.

They both had shoulder-length, jet black hair, the woman's fringe slightly longer than the man's, both had matching blue eyes that were as bright and blue as the Somerset sky outside the store.

Neither of them smiled, just sat there slowly drinking their coffees.

Then they both removed their sunglasses and started to talk to each other, in hushed tones.

The woman spoke first;

"I don't understand," she sighed, quiet enough for the man to hear but no one else, "our pick up is in Oakleigh but we're in fucking Chard, of all places!"

The man raised his hand as if to silence her, his eyelids narrowing.

"I've warned you so many times," he hissed, "stop

with the swearing. It shows a distinct lack of grace and decorum. Not to mention lack of vocabulary."

"Stop being so bloody pious all the time," she retorted, "I knew this frickin' gig was going to be a crock."

She slurped noisily at her latte and he gave her a withering look of annoyance.

She smiled, then blew him a cheeky kiss.

"So," she continued, placing he mug back upon the table between them, "why Chard?"

The man sighed and removed his sunglasses, his eyes falling upon the few patrons that were ordering at the bar, those few that were seated around them and the two female baristas, stood chatting behind the counter.

"Oakleigh is evil."

The man's voice had fallen to just above a whisper, despite no one actually listening.

The woman's smile broadened.

"I've never seen you look so serious," she laughed, her eyes darting toward the elder of the two workers behind the counter, impressed with the tightness of her brown shirt.

She licked her strawberry-coloured lips and looked back at her partner.

"So this shithole isn't?" she laughed.

"Chard has many, many faults but Oakleigh is inherently evil," the man continued, his eyes upon the same barista, impressed with her warm smile, despite the drudgery of a twelve-hour shift, "the less time we have to spend there, the better."

"I'm not complaining us being here though." the woman replied, still eyeing up the pony-tailed woman behind the counter.

"You're incorrigible," the man sighed, shaking his head, "don't you ever think of anything else than the sins of the flesh?"

It was her turn to send him a withering look, before breaking into that same, smarmy smile once again.

"It's in my nature, cousin. Blame my boss. Sometimes it's like you've only just met me," she sniggered, her eyes looking past him at the woman who was now pushing a broom around the café's floor, coming in her direction, "how long we been at this shit now?"

The man, struggling to disguise his disdain at her calling their job 'shit' and her continuing to lust over the poor, over-worked, under-paid, buxom barista, rubbed his tired eyes and finished his latte.

"As you seemingly want some sort of contact with that poor creature, why don't you go and get us a couple more drinks?" the man sighed, deciding not to pursue that particular line of conversation.

It had been a very long time.

The woman, squealing playfully, positively leapt from her seat, her grin widening as she walked quickly through the back of the cafe to the counter, exaggeratedly making the most out of squeezing past the barista, looking her up and down as she scooted back around the bar to take her order.

His partner leant upon the counter, fluttering her eyelashes, thrusting her chest forward.

He sighed, to himself this time, praying to The Father that Kushiel wouldn't loosen that white tie of hers and unbutton the top couple buttons of her black shirt.

That female, corrupted throughout time was definitely incorrigible.

Naturally.

That poor young woman, with the pretty smile, the small green eyes and the voluptuous chest, luckily, wasn't susceptible to Kush's charms, which by its own admission was pretty spectacular seeing Kushiel could charm the birds from the trees.

The devour them without a second thought, if the whim took her.

He watched her saunter back over with the tray of drinks, swinging her hips seductively from side to side as if walking upon a catwalk.

"Is she looking?" she whispered, trying not to look over her shoulder.

Zadkiel shook his head, just stopping short of noisily face-palming his head in exaggerated exasperation.

"Sit down," he hissed quietly through gritted teeth, "for once can you not try your damnedest not to draw attention to ourselves?"

Kushiel snorted derisively.

"We're sat here, in this pissant town, in conflicting, yet matching suits, drinking god-awful coffee in some crummy, coffee-chain dive, looking out of place as a nun in a whorehouse and you're worried that we may be drawing attention to ourselves? She laughed, her laughter sounding as hollow as she intended.

"You know full well they can't see our attire," he retorted as he picked up his coffee mug and grabbed the ten sugars she had picked up for him, "and I've told you, this town is lesser of the two evils."

Kushiel slid back into her chair and dragged her slender fingers through her black mane, eyeing him with as much distrust as always.

"How come we've never been here before?" she sighed, pouring in her copious amounts of brown sugar, "surely there have been cases that would have called us to a place like this throughout the millennia?"

"Chard is a bad place admittedly," he said, his voice still no more than a whisper, "but the townsfolk, despite the presence of idiotic, racist, sexist bigots that fornicate like its going out of fashion, drink themselves to oblivion almost every single night and procreate like rabbits, there has never been someone worthy of our intervention."

"It's got the obligatory corrupt town council and its sanctimonious, self-serving councillors," she stated in all seriousness, "the whiny, opinionated 'ordinary' people who are quick to condemn and point the finger when they should be looking at their own lives. Those jumped-up, sanctimonious pricks with money who think they are better than the others. The unwed mothers who sire children from numerous partners so they can live comfortably on benefits while the hard-workers struggle to make ends meet."

"None of them have ever decided to take their own lives for no reason," Zadkiel said solemnly, "and they aren't necessarily evil people. Just ignorant, ill-informed and a little self-centred. Most of them, like the people in any other town in this God-fearing country are pretty decent people."

Kushiel shook her head dismissively.

"So not one person, in the entire history of this place has been offered a chance at redemption? I cant believe that," she sighed laconically, "every town, every village, every city we've ever frequented has it's share of sycophantic, hedonistic, self-gratifying miscreants, yet Chard has never had one person who deserved The Choice?"

Zadkiel shook his head once more.

"Damn," Kushiel whistled, "this really is a shithole."

Zadkiel thought about admonishing her for her continuous uses of vulgarities but it was a good hour before they were due in Oakleigh and he'd rather keep her onside, for the time being at least.

And at least she had stopped fixating on the buxom barista.

"So," Kushiel started, "we've got an hour to kill, I assume that young lady is out of bounds..."

She left that hanging there for a second, saw Zadkiel's eyes roll, smiled yet again, then continued:

"So, what the flippity-flip are we going to do?"

Zadkiel rubbed his hairless chin thoughtfully, knowing it wouldn't really matter what they did as time is only really a human construct, created to give them the illusion of control and some semblance of normality. Himself, his kith and kin, weren't bound to such earthly restraints but somewhere deep within himself, he quite enjoyed playing along.

He even wished he got around to acquiring one of those gorgeous Vacheron Constatin Overseas watches,he'd once seen online.

There was always time, he supposed.

Smiling to himself, he looked at his companion.

"Maybe we can just sit here, drink our coffee and shoot the breeze?" Zadkiel said, "how's Lucifer?"

Kushiel exaggeratedly rolled her eyes, letting out a long sigh.

"Happy as a pig in shit," she sighed, the ironic sarcasm dripping from every word, "still got a god-damn chip on his shoulder, as always. Still unhappy that I have to do this."

"Ours is not to question Him," Zadkiel whispered in hushed tone, raising his eyes heavenward, "what he says goes."

"He's not my boss!" Kushiel protested, blowing outwards that made her lips wobble.

"Not directly, no," he replied, "but even Luce knows not to annoy him when it comes to his ideas and in all honesty, it was Lucifer's choice to send you as his envoy."

Kushiel glowered at him, indignation and realisation etched across her angelic face.

"Mammon wanted the job so be thankful you ended up with me," she replied.

"And Gabriel wanted it too, so who has more to be thankful for?"

She opened her mouth to say something else but thought better of it, choosing to pick up her coffee and sip her latte.

"I still don't understand any of this," Kushiel snapped, knowing that if she started talking about Gabriel she wouldn't be able to stop, "how can I perform to the best of my abilities if I don't know what the hell is going on?"

Zadkiel fixed her with a steely gaze, looking at her over the rim of his coffee cup.

"We are told what we need to know and that's that, you know the score Kushiel."

"But why?" she snorted.

"There is a hierarchy, Kushiel, we are ALL given a job to do, as part of God's plan and we have to get on with it, I don't sit down and complain and even though Lucifer is annoyed, he understands."

"It's all bullshit."

For the umpteenth time that day, he knew that it wouldn't be the last, he let out a long sigh and glared at his partner.

"Least you still have your wings," Zadkiel snipped, "and we don't class you guys as demons, so what really do you have to complain about?"

She bit her lip but didn't respond.

As far as she was concerned, there was a huge amount of things she could complain about but Zadkiel didn't care, wouldn't agree with her and couldn't do fuck all about any of it anyway.

She seethed inside, resisting the extremely strong urge to stand up, unfurl her wings and lay every soul in sight to waste, starting with the busty brunette with the small eyes and big heart. She caught sight of her out of the corner of her eye and felt those immoral yearnings from deep within begin to boil away. It would be so easy to take her into the toilets, defile her, with her actual consent, then tear her limb from limb if she felt like it.

It wouldn't be the first time.

But Kushiel knew that Zadkiel would intervene and stop any of that from happening.

There was a lot of unearthly talents they did actually have but luckily, angels didn't have telepathic abilities so he'd never know what her true feelings were. He just thought she wanted to fuck the woman.

What he didn't know, wouldn't hurt him.

Her smile returned, which unsettled Zadkiel slightly.

"Anyway," Kushiel resumed, "who's this guy we're after today?"

Zadkiel pulled what resembled an Amazon Fire from his jacket's inside pocket and snapped his fingers over the screen. It flickered to life and a list appeared.

"Name's Joseph Fender, 35 years old, an aspiring writer, unemployed, married to Sally for the past twenty years."

"So far so fucking boring."

"This is the last time I'm warning you Kushiel!"

She poked out her tongue impishly.

He continued;

"Has been suffering from anxiety and depression since the age of 13, has always struggled to fit in. Apparently, his wife has come to the end of her tether and is reluctantly leaving him, he believes she is the love of his life and will NOT take her leaving too well."

"So what's he planning?"

"Not that he's aware of it quite yet but it says here that he'll kill himself and take a few unsuspecting police officers with him."

"But isn't Oakleigh an evil place? Surely it can't hurt to take a few of them out?"

Zadkiel shook his head, yet again.

"That's not part of the plan, Kushiel, we have to save those people and give Mr Fender The Choice, that's it."

"He's going to absolutely love that!" she laughed, he voice rising in volume that made the rest of the customers in the shop look at the pair of them, "he's going to pitch a fit!"

"Then we will have to assist him Kushiel."

Zadkiel glanced around at the interested patrons and with a deft wave of his hand, they resumed with their inane, unimportant conversations and untroubled existences, oblivious to the pair of them in their midst.

Kushiel, cracked the knuckles of her slender fingers

and sighed with contentment.

"So, lets stop sitting here like we're some characters in a Tarantino movie and go and kick some ass!"

Zadkiel smiled slightly.

"I like to believe we're more like the cool angels in Supernatural," he said quietly, "sat in some garish, neon-drenched, dive-bar, shooting the breeze with Sam and Dean Winchester."

"You confuse the shit out of me Zad," she looked at him quizzically, unsure of how to take him half the time, "how the hell can you be as cool as to know what the fuck Supernatural is, yet be such a straight-laced, pious, up-your-own-ass, fucking sonofabitch?"

His eyes flashed red and his lips drew back to reveal a grimace that took her by surprise. She knew instinctively that she'd obviously overstepped the mark, she'd never seen him angry and knew that if she didn't apologise, there would be hell to pay.

Literally.

Vengeful angels were bad enough.

Angry ones were best avoided.

She opened her mouth to say sorry but with a wave of his other hand, the tie around her neck started to tighten and it pulled her face to within inches of his. She could see the fury in his eyes, could see the very fires of hell reaching toward the heavens within the irises. It was quite spectacular, unnerving, terrifying but spectacular nonetheless.

"I consider rage such a human emotion," he growled menacingly, grabbing hold of her tie and tightening it further, "but if you EVER talk to me like that again, refer to me as anything other than Zadkiel, then I will pull off your wings like some damn insect and cast you back to the depths with the rest of your damned brethren."

"If there's going to be any trouble, I'm going to have to ask you to leave."

Zadkiel and Kushiel turned their heads.

The buxom barista, with Patty on her name-tag, was stood before them, her hands on her hips, fixing them with her own steely glare that wouldn't have looked out of place on Zadkiel's face.

Zadkiel looked into her eyes and took a great deal of notice of the indignation and seriousness nestled there.

Kushiel looked at Patty's chest and wanted those brown buttons on her uniform's shirt to pop loose.

"We apologise, er, Patty," Kushiel said sweetly, her beaming smile returning as Zadkiel released her tie and she made a point of staring at Patty's name-tag as she spoke, "high spirits for a couple of youngsters like ourselves. It wont happen again."

"That's good, you shouldn't make me angry, you wouldn't like me when I'm angry!" Patty laughed in mock seriousness, giving a half-serious growl while flexing her biceps.

"Incredible Hulk," Zadkiel said quietly, watching her walk away.

"You see what I mean..." Kushiel started but silenced herself quickly as his withering glare, the one he'd seemingly used all god-damn day, made sure she didn't repeat her mistake from a few seconds ago.

She wouldn't labour her point.

"I like this town." Kushiel stated, her smile returning as she watched Patty's shapely backside as she walked away, "we coming back here at all?"

Zadkiel shook his head but shrugged his shoulders also.

"No idea but you never know."

He then caught sight of Kushiel leering over the woman again and rolled his eyes yet again., wanting so much to lean across and clip her across the ear as if he were a parent admonishing a petulant schoolchild.

He managed to resist the urge.

But only just.

"Time for us to go," he sighed, "put your eyes back

HEAVEN OR HELL

into your head and let's get out of here."

Kushiel feigned disappointment and laughed as she got to her feet, reaching for her large overcoat. She kept her eyes on curvy Patty as the two of them made their way through the coffee shop, the customers beginning to fill the place as school had kicked out, pupils and parents finding their way to Costa.

A few of them looked at the two of them, a couple, pretty, middle-aged mothers casting admiring glances, a few giggling school-girls looking them up and down.

Patty saw the young couple get up from their seats at the back of the store and smiled to herself as the young woman kept her eyes on her. She had seen the wanton looks the black-haired woman had been giving her for the past 45 minutes and although she was straight, Patty found herself wanting her. She couldn't put her finger on it but it seemed that every time the woman looked at her, Patty felt a stirring in her loins, akin to a burning sensation though not as painful as that sounded. More pleasurable than painful, if she was honest.

And she wanted more.

Patty watched the two of them amble through the store, coming closer with each careful step, the young woman with eyes on her, the young man, his eyes on the rest of the shop's customers. The two of them were what Patty classed as 'brutally handsome', neither would look out of place in a magazine or on a catwalk, perfect, high cheek bones, piercing blue eyes, chiselled chins.

She wasn't used to seeing such beautiful people in Chard.

So naturally, they stood out like a sore thumb.

That wasn't to say that the town was full of ugly people, just no one was as beautiful as these two. Her new boyfriend, Ivan was a pretty handsome guy, a Polish national, new to the town but he paled into insignificance next to this pair.

Yet it was the woman that fascinated her, the woman that she ached for, the woman that she would be thinking of when she rode Ivan like a woman possessed later that evening.

As Patty wiped down the counter, the pair of them drew level and she found herself wanting to leap unartistically over the counter and upon the woman who smiled a devilish smile and winked suggestively at her.

Patty though she would faint there and then, feeling that same unnerving heat spread down below.

"Be seeing you." the woman said, the point of her tongue poking from the corner of her mouth salaciously.

Patty shuddered involuntarily.

Her hand went instinctively to her throat, mentally saying the words "oh my goodness" as they walked out of the door, closing her eyes momentarily as what she could only describe as a 'mini orgasm' powered through her.

The man and the woman faded into nothing before the door closed, seemingly blinking out of existence as a small cloud blotted out the sun over head, the first small drops of rain beginning to fall upon the town.

Within minutes it was a downpour, the glorious summer day descending into greyness as the rain washed the streets of Chard clean

HEAVEN OR HELL

JUSTIN CHARLES MASON

BLESS HER COTTON SOCKS

Father Roger MacKenzie rapped loudly upon the red front door of number 27 and shuffled his feet while waiting for the occupants to answer. It was a brisk, cool, March morning and the sun was struggling to creep out from behind a rather nasty-looking grey cloud that hung ominously over the town but he wasn't cold. In fact, he was beginning to wish he hadn't worn his heavy overcoat, when leaving the rectory half an hour earlier.

For the short walk through the town to the housing estate of Petter's Drive, he had navigated Bodley Street, Main Street and King's Road with relative briskness, stopping to doff his hat to passing parishioners and wish them a very good morning, whether they were members of his church or not.

He considered himself a progressive vicar, at tune with the modernisation of the Church, very pro-active and a more than upright pillar of the community.

Even though he considered Oakleigh a positively evil den of iniquity, full of godless heathens who would sell their souls to the Devil himself to get ahead in life. Even their grandmothers if he was completely honest with himself.

It could be worse though.

He could be in Chard.

He had come to 27 St Peter's Drive to see Mr & Mrs Handford, the newest members of his congregation, a sweet, polite young couple who had moved to the town three months previous. They were young, executive types with a fair amount of money, the house they had purchased was testament to that and they had integrated themselves into this quiet neighbourhood with a certain amount of decorum and warm-heartedness that this area desperately needed.

Jessica, the petite, blonde, wife and mother, had approached Father MacKenzie that previous Sunday to ask if they could get their six year old daughter, Beth, christened. Beth hadn't been present at mass that morning which confused Roger as Micah, the father and the two other children, five year old Peter and three year old Paul had been there.

When questioned, Jessica had explained that Beth had been suffering with a cold and had been looked after by her grandparents, Wilma and Jeremy, Jessica's parents. She also explained that Beth hadn't yet been christened, even though the two boys had.

Father MacKenzie had been intrigued to say the least.

He had tried to press her on why the young girl hadn't been christened but Jessica had flitted away like a busy hummingbird, telling the vicar to come and see them the following week.

So as he rang the doorbell, he found himself wondering all over again.

The door opened and there stood a gorgeous, brown-haired young girl, no more than six years old, wearing a floral summer dress with a red ribbon in her hair. She instantly made Roger think of Snow White in the Disney classic, albeit a younger, smaller version.

She was grinning from ear to ear, her bright blue eyes positively glistening in the morning sunshine.

"Good morning young lady," Roger said in his kindest, warmest tone, "I'm Father MacKenzie."

The young girl's grin never changed but she didn't reply.

"I've come to see your mother about getting you christened," he continued, smiling down at her.

Still, she never said a word.

"Is your mother there?"

The six year old turned and skipped away down the carpeted hallway, leaving the vicar on the doorstep, tentatively he stepped inside and called out.

Jessica stuck her head around the corner, her hair up in a loose bun, flour on her flustered face and satin shirt.

"Come in Father," she shouted with a smile on her lips, "am just baking."

Roger stepped over the threshold and she emerged clutching a mixing bowl, wearing a flowery pinny over her smart clothes, looking more at home in some cheesy 50's, American sitcom than suburban South Somerset.

"Please, take off your coat. Would you like some tea?" she said, disappearing back into what he assumed was the kitchen, "come on through."

He could hear what sounded like a t.v in the far room, a Disney animated film was obviously playing, judging by the sickly-sweet, saccharine melody being sung as he walked toward where Mrs Hanford had disappeared, removing his heavy overcoat as he went. The kitchen wasn't as expansive and expensively decadent as most that he'd ever visited in this affluent area but it was tastefully decorated and outfitted with all the modern amenities. Jessica was leaning against the black faux-marble central counter, furiously stirring the mixture within the glass bowl as Beth perched herself upon a nearby stool at the matching breakfast bar.

Roger watched the young girl look up at her mother but Jessica's eyes were upon his.

"Please excuse the mess," she apologised above the

noise of the whisk against the glass, "promised the boys that us girls would make them a chocolate cake today and unfortunately, I can negotiate deal for hundreds of thousands but not decorate with them."

Her laugh was rather shrill but infectious all the same.

Roger was enchanted immediately.

Jessica winked at her daughter and the youngster responded in kind, grinning at her mother with adoration.

"She doesn't speak." Jessica said quietly, her eyes never leaving her daughters, "never has and we believe she never will."

Roger was shocked.

"We don't see it as a disability, or indeed a problem."

"Quite right too," Roger chimed in, "Corinthians 12.9 'And He has said to me, "My grace is sufficient for you, for power is perfected in weakness " Most gladly, therefore, I will rather boast about my weaknesses, so that the power of Christ may dwell in me."

Jessica nodded reverently.

Beth turned to face Roger and when he mother wasn't looking, stuck her tongue out impishly.

Obviously not a great lover of Chapter and Verse, Roger thought to himself, managing to suppress a smile at her impertinence, if indeed it was what he thought she was implying. He doubted it somewhat though, the thought of a six year old mute girl cocking her nose toward scripture seemed slightly preposterous.

"Does she possess any compensation for her loss of speech?"

Jessica shook her head dismissively.

"She is blessed with a great sense of humour if that's what you mean."

Roger didn't but didn't press it any further.

Jessica proceeded to pour the mixture from her bowl into a couple of cake trays under Beth's rapturous gaze and the two of them placed them in the warmed oven.

"Can I interest you in a coffee?"

Roger didn't need asking twice.

Jessica invited Roger into the lounge, draping her pinny over the edge of the central counter as they took their drinks with them. She ordered the boys to take Beth outside and gratefully switched off the television as the three children opened the patio doors and ran out to play in the long, green garden, bathed in glorious morning sunlight.

Roger sat upon a soft, black leather, two-seater sofa while Jessica perched daintily upon one of the two leather armchairs, her legs tucked beneath her. The two of them chatted with the sound of the children outside, laughing, whooping and hollering while they ran and played amongst the trees and bushes.

It turned out that Micah was away on business for a couple of days so Jessica had taken a few days off to spend some quality time with the children, both on her own and some time with her rather doting parents.

Roger drank his coffee, careful not to let Jessica see him admiring the curve of her calves beneath that black pencil-skirt and the way the pearls fell into the discreet cleavage of that delightful satin shirt. He considered it a bit of a perk that some of his parishioners were rather attractive. He may be a 'man of the cloth' but he wasn't dead from the neck down, even though most women probably thought he'd never look at them in that way.

Jessica was no different, she only saw a dog-collar.

Roger however saw how high and pert her chest was, how bountiful and rounded her backside was, the redness of her cheeks, the lustre of her brown eyes and her long, blonde hair.

Then, he caught sight of Beth stood in the doorway, her eyes upon him, the smile on her face replaced with disdain and dislike.

Roger, coughed, choking on his coffee and when he regained his composure, he looked up.

Beth wasn't there any more.

"Anyway," he coughed, "how does this coming Sunday sound for the Christening? I know it's short notice but I have another ceremony already scheduled so I could tack you onto the end."

Jessica squealed with delight, clapping her hands gleefully.

"That would be amazing!" she laughed excitedly, "Micah will be so pleased, he's been on about getting Beth named officially for an absolute age."

"Why have you not Christened her before now?" Roger decided to ask, the question had been on his mind and he could see not reason not to ask it now the Christening had been finalised.

Jessica put her coffee cup down upon the glass coffee-table and rubbed what appeared to be an aching neck, sighing as she kneaded her flesh.

"We have tried," she said quietly, glancing at the three children playing in the garden, "but events seem to conspire against us getting it actually done."

Roger raised an eyebrow quizzically as he placed his empty cup beside Jessica's.

"We have tried on three separate occasions," she continued, "the first time we had an car accident, a blow-out on the A303."

Roger nodded sagely, knowing that these things, however unfortunate, always happen when you least expect, or merit them.

"The second time, Peter ended up in hospital after swallowing one of those damn toy soldiers and we nearly lost him."

Roger stopped nodding and studied her demeanour, her eyes welling with tears that threatened to spill, the words catching in her throat.

"Lastly, my mother, Wilma, suffered a minor heart-attack on the morning of the third attempt, it wasn't too serious but we felt that God was telling us Beth shouldn't be christened."

Roger leant forward and placed his hand upon Jessica's, feeling hers tremble beneath his.

"He may work in mysterious ways and ultimately may test us every now and then but I can assure you, my dear, that he would welcome little Beth into his Church willingly and gladly."

It was then that he noticed that Beth was missing from the family portrait, within the gilded photo-frame that sat upon the table adjacent to Jessica's armchair. And quickly glancing around the room, he could see that there were no pictures of Beth at all. There were pictures of Jessica and Micah, pictures of her with the boys, Micah with the boys, pictures of Peter and Paul together.

Jessica caught sight of him looking at the assorted pictures dotted around the lounge.

"Beth doesn't like having her photo taken," she said softly, her eyes filling with tears yet again, "we have tried but she is quite stubborn when she wants to be."

Roger thought that the little madam had far too much sway with her family and if she was his daughter, she'd be bloody forced to do what she was bloody told.

But he would never say as much.

"I will see you in church this Sunday," he said calmly, his fingers encircling hers, "we'll get little Beth christened, finally."

That evening, sitting in his favourite, tattered, yet extremely comfortable leather armchair, he sipped from his large glass of red wine, smoking his pipe, with his slipper-covered feet perched up upon the matching and equally battered footstool. He had Radio 4 on in the background, a current affairs comedy programme lampooning the incompetent American President, which although quite humorous, he found a little contrite and laboured. He wasn't really paying attention, his thoughts dwelling upon Jessica Hanford and her mute daughter.

He found the thought of her a little unsettling; her

precocious demeanour, her parent's apparent lack of discipline with the child, the rather strange lack of any pictures of the girl. And those attempts at getting the girl christened.

He couldn't quite put his finger on it but there was something about the child that worried him.

And he hoped that nothing would happen to derail that Christening on Sunday. He took great pride in his church, in it's undertakings and its standing within the town of Oakleigh.

Sitting within his snug, cluttered lounge, surrounded by scores of dusty, dog-eared books upon wooden bookshelves, scattered papers and half-written sermons upon his writing desk in the corner, Roger sipped from his glass of wine and pondered what he could tell his congregation of little Beth Hanford.

Jessica held the iPhone to her ear as she poured herself a sizeable glass of white wine, standing in the now-clean kitchen, a little after 10pm. The kids were asleep upstairs, she had put all three of them to bed a little before 8pm and had spent the last two hours tidying the house from top to bottom.

She would be the first to admit that it was a little bizarre to clean at that time but she found it easier with the children out of the way and keeping them occupied for most of the day was exhilarating and demanding in equal measure. She loved them with all that she was but working three days a week gave her the break from them that she needed.

She was trying to call Micah but he wasn't answering.

Annoyed, she threw down the phone upon the kitchen counter and sipped from her glass of wine.

She never saw a dark flurry of movement in the hallway.

Jessica heard a faint creak upon the staircase and walked slowly to the kitchen doorway, craning her head to listen out for anything else.

There was nothing.

She stepped into the hallway and looked upwards.

The stairs were empty.

She glanced into the lowly-lit lounge and apart from shadows cast upon the walls, there seemed to be nothing there.

Looking back up the stairs, she walked slowly upon the carpeted hallway, her bare feet making no sound. She toyed nervously with the string of pearls she wore around her neck as she stepped upon the bottom stair, the wine sloshing gently in her tightly-held glass. As she ascended the stairs, she held onto the bannister rail, her eyes upon the landing up ahead. She half expected one of the kids to emerge from their rooms but by the time she got to the top, none of them had sprung into view. Being as quiet as she could, she peeked into the boy's room first.

Both Peter and Paul were crashed out, Peter, in his Iron Man pyjamas was tangled in his bedsheets as usual, Paul in his Spiderman onesie, hanging half in and half out of his wooden bed, his bare bum on show.

Jessica put her glass down upon the white chest of drawers and gently, tenderly helped Paul back into bed, kissing him upon his brow and tucking him under his sheets. Backing out of the room, she carefully picked up her glass and quietly shut their door.

Beth's bedroom door was ajar and Jessica could see the night-light plugged in just inside.

Trying to be as quiet as possible, she pushed the door open, an inch at a time.

Beth was sat up in bed, her arms crossed over her chest, her dark eyes staring right at Jessica, a look of pure venom upon her face.

Jessica gasped, dropping her glass, her other hand clutching her throat, her heart leaping into her mouth.

"Oh honey." she gasped, "you scared mummy. Why aren't you asleep sweetheart?"

Beth glared at her, chewing on her bottom lip angrily.

"Do you want mummy to tuck you in?"

Jessica took a step toward the bed.

Beth glared harder, her eyes narrowing and her brow lowering.

Jessica stopped in her tracks, feeling an ache starting behind her left eye that resembled the onset of a migraine whilst feeling a light tickle in the back of her throat.

"OK sweetheart," she stammered, feeling light-headed all of a sudden, "Mummy is feeling a little woozy, Mummy thinks she needs to get to bed."

Jessica thought about kissing Beth goodnight but her breath was a little short and the headache seemed to be intensifying so crouching, she retrieved her fallen glass and backed out, not raising her eyes to her clearly irate daughter.

She suddenly got the urge to go and have a bath, the thought seemingly leaping into her mind and she started to unbutton her blouse as she walked absent-mindedly toward the bathroom at the end of the landing.

As Jessica peeled off her blouse, she reached into the bath and plugging it, she turned on the taps.

Beth was stood in her bedroom's doorway, watching her mother, her arms still folded across her chest.

Glaring angrily as her mother slipped off her underwear and stepped into the bath.

Roger jerked awake, the radio still playing in the background, his neck hurting something chronic as he'd fallen asleep, yet again, at a funny angle. His joints creaked nosily as he straightened himself while prone in his chair, his onset of rheumatism giving him that familiar and unwelcome aching he had come to dread.

He glanced at the wall clock and sighed as he read that it was a little after 1am, cursing the fact he'd fallen asleep in the chair and would regret it when he had to rise so early that coming morning. He rose from the chair, his bones creaking and his pains making him wince, reaching to turn off the radio before he padded softly upon the wooden floorboards, nearly, for the umpteenth time tripping upon the frayed edge of his Persian rug, making his way to the light-switch by the door.

He stopped in his tracks as he heard a small scurrying sound coming from the adjacent hallway and what at first sounded like the strains of children laughter. He looked around at the radio, hoping that it was just some trick of the gloom that had made the sound appear that it had come from the hallway.

He then remembered her had just switched the radio off.

Roger turned on the main lounge light, blinking to become accustomed to the brightness after the semi-darkness he had awoken in.

Then heard some more scurrying further along the hall.

He threw open the lounge door and scrambling for the light-switch in the hall, he held his breath as the bulb cast its illumination.

The hall was empty.

Sighing loudly, puffing out his cheeks with relief, he stood there for a moment, thinking what an old fool he was, scared by the creaking of the old house in the dead of the night.

He then heard what sounded like some more creaking at the top of the stairs and glancing upwards, he thought he saw a flash of movement in the corner of his eye., something small, something dark, something fast.

He was afraid.

"Who's there?" he stammered, holding onto the door-frame to hold him up, his legs threatening to buckle beneath him, "I'll call the police!"

The unmistakeable tinkling sound of light, children's laughter came from the ventilation grate next to the lounge door.

Whomever it was, they were in his bedroom directly overhead.

Roger stood shivering in the hall's doorway and reached into his gown's pocket to retrieve his trusty Nokia 3310, the mobile he'd had for ages. He punched in 999 and went to press the call button when he heard a few words in the grate, words that wafted down from upstairs.

"Father...father...help me, I'm lost...help me."

It sounded like a little girl, yet there seemed to be malice dripping from every word, an underlying evil in each sickly little word, a breathless, simpering terror in each spoken syllable.

Then came the laughter, wispy, ethereal and as he found it, nerve-shredding callous.

Roger took a step toward the bottom of the staircase, his thumb hovering above the call button of the battered old Nokia, his breath catching in his throat.

There came a loud bang from overhead and then a rumbling noise, sounding very much to Roger like someone had jumped off of his springy bed and was running out of his room toward the landing.

But the sound was deafening, sounding like a herd of elephants trumpeting across his head.

He stepped out into the hallway, half expecting for someone to appear at the top of the stairs as the sound came closer.

Clutching the bottom of the bannister her peered upwards, the blood thundering in his ears, his heart beating a staccato beat within his breast, all the colour draining from his sallow, wrinkled face.

Nothing materialised at the top of the stairs.

"I'm calling the police!" he shouted, looking down at the phone still clutched in his sweaty palm and pressed the green call button.

The phone went blank.

The lights throughout the house flickered momentarily then plinked out.

Roger suddenly felt something dangle past his face and his eyes widened in terror as he felt a roped cord slipping around his head before it dug into the soft flesh of his wrinkled neck, yanking him off his feet. His hands went to the constricting rope as he dangled off the ground, trying desperately to claw at it's rough fibres as his body's weight tightened the noose around his neck. He was suspended between the thick, wooden bannisters, his slippers falling off his kicking feet, his back smacking against the wood as he dangled.

As blackness clawed at him, he could feel someone's head come through the bannister, feeling a face inches from his own, feeling hot, fetid breath in his ear. Something wet and leathery slid up his wet cheek and as the last of his breath valiantly tried to leave his body, he came face to face with a small, white face that he instantly recognised.

And big, brown, puppy-dog eyes that stared through his very soul, venomous hatred burning deep within the dark irises, flecks of bright red dancing before his eyes.

Breathing his last, Father Roger Mackenzie realised that his god had deserted him in his hour of need. He had been worshipping the wrong deity all this time.

Someone else was obviously guiding this pitiful life, his pitiful life.

And he had been found wanting.

The devil walked among them.

And wore a colourful summer dress.

And a bright red ribbon in black ringlets.

Micah Hanford had driven back to Oakleigh at break-neck speed, the phone-call from Jessica's parents that morning still hadn't managed to break through. He drove almost on auto-pilot, breaking the speed limit regularly while negotiating the A303 but not caring at all.

He had to get home.

His car almost flew through the air as he drove over the southern bridge that straddled the bottom of the town, passing the factories, the school, the houses in a blur in his windscreen as he tore through Oakleigh's streets. The car screeched into St Peter's Drive.

There were two police cars parked outside number 27, an ambulance and a silver Mondeo he immediately recognised as Jessica's parents, Wilma and Jeremy.

Jeremy's words seemingly floated into his befuddled mind, the phone call he had received an hour and a half earlier burning in his his brain;

"You need to come home...there's been an accident."

Micah leapt from the car as it screeched to a halt, running toward the door of his home when he caught sight of Wilma and Jeremy in the back of the ambulance. His heart leapt into his mouth as he saw Peter, Paul and Beth stood by the side of the ambulance, all three dressed in their nightclothes and dressing-gowns, shivering in the cold.

He ran to them, scooping all three up into his big, strong arms, burying his face in their small chests, their bodies racking with small sobs. Wilma was being attended to by a female paramedic, being given what looked like oxygen through a surgical mask. Jeremy held her hand attentively, dried tears upon his blustered cheeks, soothing words trying desperately to calm her down.

A tall brown-haired woman and an extremely large uniformed policeman emerged from the front door of his house and approached Micah and the children.

"Mr Hanford?" the woman said softly, "I'm Detective Sam King, could we have a word in private please?"

Micah nodded, putting down the three children and shepherding them toward Jeremy who had stepped down from the ambulance with open arms.

The large policeman never said a word and ushered Micah and the police woman to one side with a wave of his colossal arm, the two of them standing to the side of the front door as the uniformed officer stood guard.

"I'm afraid there has been an accident," the detective sighed, placing a hand upon his arm, her brown eyes full of sincerity and reverence, "it's your wife, Jessica."

"Where is she?" Micah growled, his heart sinking once more, his ragged voice faltering as he spoke.

He heard movement inside and as he looked into the hallway, he could see two men in white coats coming down the stairs, carrying a black bag upon a black stretcher; a black, body-sized bag.

Micah felt his legs buckle, imagined vomit and bile rising up from his gullet, the world starting to swim before his eyes. Samantha King, with almost super-human speed, caught hold of him as he stumbled where he stood, her slender fingers gripping his arm in a vice-like grip that certainly belied her strength considerably.

"There was nothing anyone could do," the woman sighed, holding him up against the outer wall of the house as the men and the stretcher emerged into the cool, sunny morning air, "your wife had died sometime during the night."

Micah pitched to the side and tried to vomit but the lack of substance meant nothing came, his dry, hacking attempts at puking, loud amongst the silence of the morning.

Jeremy had covered the children's faces as the body-bag had been removed from the house and placed carefully into a black midi-van that was parked to the far side of the road.

Micah watched them close the door and drive away, tears streaming down his face, the world swimming before his eyes, the woman's fingers still digging into his arm as she held him up.

"How?" he stammered, "how did she die?"

The police woman relinquished her grip on his arm and straightened the front of her blue suit's jacket, running her fingers through her lengthy hair.

"We will wait for the coroner's report," she sighed, her dark eyes looking up at him, "but early indications point to the possibility your wife drowned."

Micah, wiping away the tears from his blood-shot eyes, stared at her sullenly.

"Drowned?" his question was disbelieving, almost accusing, the incredulity in his voice almost palatable.

"Your wife was discovered naked, upstairs in the empty bath."

"Who found her?"

"Your daughter, Mr Hanford, she apparently awoke her brothers and they called your father-in-law, before informing us. That's some spunky kids you have there. They're going to need you to be strong, Mr Hanford."

Micah had stopped listening, his attention was on the three children who Jeremy was sheltering by the side of the ambulance, those brave, wonderful children who had found their mother dead and had the forethought to call their grandfather and an ambulance.

He wished he had been there for them, for all of them, he knew he could have saved Jessica, he could have been there so none of this would have happened.

He would never leave them again.

Jeremy bundled the three kids into the Mondeo, Micah had gone to the mortuary to formally identify Jessica, Wilma had been heavily sedated and taken to the hospital as a precaution.

He drove them across town to their farm at the north of Oakleigh, past the chapel ruins on the hill, out through the light-dappled country lanes that overlooked the town.

After pulling into the gravelled driveway that led to the pristine farmhouse, the kids had ambled inside, the boys holding his hand, Beth skipping through the open door.

He watched her skip through the flagstone hallway and plonk herself upon the cloth sofa in front of the flat-screen t.v. She reached for the remote control and flicked on the Disney Channel.

He was amazed by her resilience in the face of overwhelming, heart-breaking adversity, the death of her mother would scar her for the rest of her life.

It broke his heart.

Beth turned her head to look at him, a smile plastered on her pretty, porcelain-coloured, angelic face, her red ribbon shining brightly within her black ringlets as the sun poured in through the bay-window.

Her smile never faded as she turned back to face the screen, the animation obviously delighting her as the words of the uplifting, powerful song filled the room to the rafters.

Her smile would be there for a long time to come.

THE BIKE DEAL

The woman sat in the cafe, reading a folded newspaper while sipping from a china tea-cup, her left leg across her right knee.

She wore a cerise pink and black, skirt-suit above a white collarless blouse, her long, slender legs encased in sheer stockings, black, six-inch heels upon her feet.

She wore the bare minimum of make-up: a little foundation, a smidgen of lipstick, a dab of mascara. There were diamond studs in her dainty ears, a plethora of silver, gold and tungsten ringers upon various fingers and a single, solid gold chain disappearing into the opening of the front of her blouse.

She wore black, designer spectacles, perched daintily upon her pert, small nose that she looked over the rims at her newspaper, her light blue eyes darting across the written page.

She had high cheek bones, a thinnish, oval face that ended in a soft, dimpled chin, full, pouting lips, thin, dark eyebrows that gave her the look of deep thought as she read.

Her name was Tabitha Williams, she was the owner of the cafe that she was currently sat in and she was waiting for 10am.

She had an appointment at the bank in Oakleigh that morning, an appointment with the manager, Sarah, to discuss the overdraft that Tabby had steadily gone over, month after month. The business was haemorrhaging money like crazy and despite her rather expensive skirt-suit, her expensive looking jewellery and her posturing, Tabby was flat broke.

The property in Oakleigh's bustling Main Street, had been in her family for what seemed generations; her family having a presence in Oakleigh since the 1800's, had purchased the small building back at the turn of the century and it had been in previous incarnations, a haberdashery, an ironmongers and since 1964, a cafe.

Tabby's mother, Irene had passed it onto her upon her passing in 1998 and though Tabby had loathed it at the time, she had kept the business afloat, hoping in turn that when she died, she could let her children inherit it.

Now there was a danger she was going to lose the whole shebang and if she didn't stem the leak, the whole dam was certain to break.

Her eldest daughter,twenty-two-year-old Emily, didn't give a shit about the cafe, caring more about her blossoming career as a barmaid at The Hangman's Arms pub, a hundred yards up the road. Her next two, Una and Fiona, at the age of eighteen and seventeen, respectively, were still slaving away in school and college, forging careers in sports development and journalism. Her youngest, Amelia, at the age of twelve was too young to even help out now and again, though Tabby would let her work the till when she was particularly quiet. Which was more often than not nowadays.

Most of the time, Tabby couldn't give two hoots about leaving her daughter's her legacy but lately she had been taking stock of her life and had decided that it wasn't the girl's fault that the business was failing so couldn't blame it on their lackadaisical approach to the business.

THE BIKE DEAL

She had started to look closer to home.

Tabby realised that even if there was a cash injection into her livelihood, she couldn't make the punters come through the door. Oakleigh's town centre was dying on its arse and times were hard in this town. Even Chard, despite some of the arseholes that lived there, had green shoots of revival beginning to poke through. The talk of the 'Chard Regeneration' had galvanised most of the townsfolk into positive thinking, even though there was a '20 year plan' that some were more than sceptical about. But Chard was at least looking to the future, no matter how misguided and possibly fruitless it may turn out to be.

Oakleigh was so stuck in the past, Tabby half expected for farmers to start moving their cattle through the streets, rag and bone men to travel by horse and cart through the roads and horse-drawn stagecoaches to rattle through the cobbled streets on their way to London. Every now and then, she could imagine women in long dresses, men in breeches, waistcoats and top-hats promenading through Oakleigh like some Victorian-style picture postcard.

She knew that most towns were struggling to get customers through their shop's doors, the internet and online shopping had sounded it's death knell for years now but she truly believed that if she could expand, plough more money into the business, that she would survive.

Tabby's cooked breakfasts had always been the talk of the town, loved by various hard-working workmen, postmen and women on their way home, school kids on their way to the Comprehensive, even members of the local constabulary, all came to taste her wares. She would be the first to admit that she loved to flirt outrageously with the burly men, to mother and mollycoddle the children and gossip like a fishwife with the women but she saw it as her keeping everyone satisfied, happy and content.

Unfortunately, she had a tendency to go a little too

far every now and again, which upset certain people at certain times and her reputation, though not the highest by any stretch of the imagination, had taken a few hits over the years.

There had been the sexual conquest of a seventeen year old friend of Fiona's, which had mortified her middle daughter to the extent that they were barely talking.

There had been the violent fight with the mother of said sexual conquest, in The Hangman's Arms, one Saturday evening not long ago, when the woman had suffered an extremely nasty cut to her face when Tabby attacked her.

There had been a few whispers of Tabby constantly taking home one man after the other, even apparently two in one night, for loud love-making or loud arguments that shocked and annoyed the neighbours in equal measure.

Tabby was known around town as a vicious drunk, a woman of low virtue, a woman who had four different children by four different fathers, vindictive, cold-hearted and would fuck any man with a pulse who would glance in her direction.

Tabby didn't give a flying fuck what anyone thought of her, she never had and she never would, all she cared about was her mother's cafe.

She would get on her bended knee before Sarah if she had to, she'd beg for the money, she'd offer her heart, body and soul to ensure her cafe could stay open.

Tabby read the newspaper but was just praying that something would go her way, something would help her to keep this business afloat.

Prayed that someone or something could save her.

As she sighed to herself, Tabby heard the bell above the entrance chime and glancing up from her paper, she caught sight of a tall, dark-haired woman enter the cafe.

This woman looked vaguely familiar but Tabby couldn't put a name to the rather pretty face, there seemed to be a name on the tip of her tongue but every time she thought she had it, it scampered away like mist in the wind.

The tall woman, was dressed in a black trouser-suit, a crimson satin shirt and shoe-lace tie that wouldn't have looked out of place on a cowboy. She carried a long, black, raincoat in the crook of her arm and a black, leather briefcase in her gloved hands. Her slicked-back hair was black as onyx, her round eyes the colour of emeralds, her pale skin fairer than the freshly fallen snow that lined the winter streets beyond the door.

The woman looked directly at Tabby and a smile spread across her thin, ruby-red lips.

Tabby returned the smile, still trying to recollect the woman's name.

"Ms. Williams," the woman's voice positively purred with an accent that Tabby couldn't place, though it did sound a little foreign, "Ms. Tabitha Williams? Proprietor of this fine, welcoming establishment?"

Tabby nodded, placing her newspaper on the table as she rose to her feet, straightening her skirt as she walked toward the dark-haired woman.

"Yes," Tabby said softly, "I am she."

The woman held out her hand in welcome and as Tabby's soft fingers encircled the outstretched hand, she was struck by how cold the woman's extremity was.

"Please forgive the lack of warmth in my fingers," the woman said, her eyes looking deep into Tammy's, "its a devilishly cold day out there today."

Tabby nodded, smiling, even though the woman didn't give any indication she was going to let go of her hand anytime soon. Tabby felt iciness creeping up from her wrist as if the woman was turning her to ice with each passing second but there was a warmth in the woman's green eyes that heated Tabby to her core.

"May I trouble you for a coffee?" the woman said, motioning for them to sit back down at Tabby's table, "something warm to light the fire within?"

Tabby, her high heeled shoes clacking noisily upon the hard tiles of the cafe, walked to the coffee pot and poured the woman a large mug of piping hot, black coffee. Carrying it back over, the woman took it by the outside of the mug but didn't flinch at the heat that must have burnt her fingers. Tabby sat back down opposite and looked at the woman in more detail.

She was a woman of no more than thirty-five, no make-up, no jewellery, no band upon her wedding finger. There were no labels upon her clothes though they looked more expensive than the ones Tabby herself was wearing, the cut of her trouser-suit gave her a slightly androgynous appearance but Tabby did catch a glimpse of a possible curve upon the woman's chest as she sat down.

The woman looked at her and Tabby could have sworn she had looked her up and down, here eyes darting toward the opening of her shirt, Tabby could have sworn this rather attractive woman was checking her out.

"My name is Natasha," the woman said suddenly, "and I have come here today to offer you some assistance."

Tabby was taken aback by the woman's forthrightness and determined demeanour, the woman leaning forward in her chair as if she was attempting to intimidate Tabby.

"Did Sarah send you?" Tabby stammered, the woman staring deeply into her eyes, the tip of her tongue darting from the corner of her thin lips.

The woman shook her head.

"This 'Sarah' definitely did not send me," the woman snorted, "i have come here under my own validation today to offer you my assistance."

Tabby raised a quizzical eyebrow, not dissimilar to the former wrestler, Dwayne 'The Rock' Johnson when he was doing his ring promos and pieces to camera. Tabby's kids loved the WWE shows but hated her rendition of 'The People's Eyebrow'.

"Where did you come from?" Tabby asked, "who are you?"

The woman shushed her with a hiss of derision from her lips and a wave for her dismissive hand.

"I am offering to assist your good self with a cash injection but there a couple of provisos, a few quid pro quos."

That saying nestled somewhere in the back of her mind but for the life of her, Tabby couldn't remember where she had heard that being said somewhere before.

"Do you have somewhere private we can go to discuss the details?"

Tabby nodded.

"Be a dear and lock the premises, I don't wish to be disturbed while I lay it on the line for you."

Tabby, thinking and feeling that this all sounded very unreal and somewhat familiar, locked the front door to the cafe and led the tall woman through to the back office.

The woman waited for Tabby to enter the room and shut the door behind her, turning the key in the lock.

"There," the woman sighed, urging for Tabby to take her seat with a wave of her hand while she sat on the edge of the desk, slipping off her suit jacket and rolling up the satin sleeves of her crimson blouse, "now we wont be disturbed."

Tabby saw various, brightly colourful tattoos upon the woman's forearms, both front and back; words in a foreign language laying amongst exotic looking flowers, various heads of men and women, all with piercing red eyes that seemed to follow you around the room, winged serpents and dragons that seemed to have a life of their own upon the woman's flesh.

She saw that the woman had undone the top two buttons of her shirt to reveal the tops of high, rounded breasts that seemed to defy gravity and any ravages of age. Tabby couldn't figure out how she had thought the woman looked androgynous, by any stretch of the imagination.

It must have been the cut of her expensive clothes that had given off the illusion.

"Now Tabitha, my dear," the woman said with a devilish grin, a flash of mischief in those bright, emerald eyes, "i will ensure that this delightful enterprise of yours continues to flourish within this town but this is not going to be a straight-forward business transaction, in the strictest sense of the phrase."

Tabby felt the woman's eyes boring through hers, watched the rise and fall of her breasts with each deep, laboured breath, saw the woman's lips part and the tip of her tongue flick once more at the corner of those thin lips.

"I'm as liberal as the next gal," Tabby laughed, "but I draw the line at sexual favours for money, lady."

The woman moved with unmeasurable speed and suddenly her face was inches from Tabby's, her hot breath on Tabby's face, her hands upon Tabby's.

"You say that, my dear," the woman hissed, a sly grin on her lips, "but you've fucked your way through the male population of this town for nothing less. You've sucked, snorted, fucked and blown your way through Oakleigh with such carefree abandon and disregard for your poor children that you are known as the 'Town Bike' are you not? You have the morals of an alley-cat and don't give a fuck who you've stepped over and on to get where you are today."

Tabby rose from her chair, indignant, hurt by this woman's cruel jibes, the sting of tears pricking behind the eyes.

"How dare you?" Tabby cried, wanting to grab this woman by the throat and choke the life out of her, "how fucking dare you!"

The woman tutted and putting a hand on Tabby's chest, she seemingly sent a volt of electricity through her fingertips, Tabby stumbling backwards, landing with a thump back in her chair as is she had been punched square in the chest.

"My dear, dear Tabitha," the woman cooed, running a finger down Tabitha's blouse, snagging the thick, gold chin with a perfectly manicured, yet long, painted fingernail, "methinks the lady doth protest too much."

Sullenly Tabby looked up at her.

"I do not care who you have fucked in the past my dear, I do not care what you have done to get by in this festering, shithole of a town. I do not care that your indignation burns within your callous, black heart as you lie about your reputation or your social standing."

Tabby felt a prickly heat coursing through her torso from where the woman had 'touched' her, sliding down between her breasts, down her abdomen, snaking between her thighs.

"From now on, you will continue with your wanton, debauched, hedonistic lifestyle but every month, you will bring me a sacrifice, the soul of a man, or a woman, to the chapel ruins on the hill."

Tabby looked at the woman incredulously, not understanding what the woman was actually on about, fear, indecision and a gnawing pain in the pit of her stomach choking off any response she may have rendered.

"Put simply, my dear Tabitha, you must pay me for what you desire the most, with what I desire the most."

"Are you the Devil?" Tabitha stammered, her eyes as big as saucers.

The woman chuckled beneath her breath, fixing Tabby with a withering glare that froze her heart and turned the blood in her veins to ice-water.

"No Tabitha, I am not the Devil. Just one of his underlings. As are you now."

Tabby watched the woman put on her jacket after rolling down her sleeves and straightening her shirt collar, she buttoned up her satin shirt and stood before Tabby, a wry smile on her face.

The woman sighed aggressively, pulled Tabby to her feet by the lapels of her skirt-suit's jacket then kissed her fully on the lips, wrapping her arms around Tabby's neck, pulling her close., their chests squashed hard against each other.

Tabby's eyes flicked open to find herself alone in her back office, her body tingling, heat emanating from the front of her blouse and for the life of her, she could not remember how she came to be in that office. Her lips tingled as if she had come in from the cold outside to greet the heat of her cafe but she could not remember anything apart from the fact she was meeting Sarah, from the bank, at 10am.
She emerged from the back office, the cafe was locked up but there was hot coffee in the pot and her folded up newspaper on one of the tables.
Tabby heard a faint knocking and looking up, she could see her waitress, 55 year-old former rock-chick, Christy and her cook, 45 year-old Polish national, Andre standing at the door, waiting to be let in as they shivered outside in the snow. She looked down at her iWatch and saw it was a little after 9.30am, the cafe should have been open an hour ago and she couldn't, for the life of her, think why she had left it so late.
She could remember dressing like an executive, in her pink and black skirt-suit earlier that morning, wanting to impress Sarah but couldn't remember anything after that.
Tabby let her workers in, not bothering to apologise for leaving them out in the cold, she had other things on her mind as they sauntered past her and got to work while she stood gazing out of the open door.
There was nagging thought, rattling around somewhere with the deepest recesses of her mind, an itch that just needed to scratch, an almost intense burning deep within her.
Tabby stood looking out of her cafe window, feeling her slender body aching from head to toe. She could feel the soft caress of the satin of her blouse against her soft

skin, the tightness of her jacket at her high breasts, the clinging silk of her stockings upon her long, svelte legs.

And an intense, burning longing that she wanted and needed a man.

The meeting with Sarah had been a resounding success, the bank had authorised a substantial overdraft extension and when Tabby had impudently asked, a sizeable loan had been given by Sarah that meant the cafe would be safe for a few years to come.

Tabby had decided to celebrate that evening, preferring to sample the atmosphere and ambiance of The Griffon public house, further down Main Street towards the bottom half of the town, near the police station and the trading estate. It was far enough away from The Hangman's Arms for Tabby not to think about Emily, though she doubted that the little madam gave a shit what her mother was celebrating, or indeed where.

She turned up with her close friend, Naomi, the two of them wearing short skirts and tight tops that left very little to the imagination, despite the cold, snowy town outside. Dark haired Tabby and blonde haired Naomi both had a few drinks at Tabby's spacious semi-detached house on Bodley Street, before descending upon the poor unsuspecting locals in The Griffon, whooping and hollering like a couple of drunk teenagers. The nice gay couple behind the bar, owners George and Gary, threw outrageous parties in the upstairs every Friday night, so both women headed up there as the night wore on.

Before too long, Tabby was dancing on the sweaty dance-floor, grinding herself against an equally drunk male, his hands on her curves, his tongue tying hers in knots. She laughed uncontrollably, feeling alive for the first time in ages, energy coursing through her body like wildfire as the pounding music filled her ears, the man's hands kneading her, his hot breath upon her face, her neck, her mouth.

Tabby let the man have his way with her in the alley behind the pub; it wasn't dignified, it wasn't particularly pleasurable and it definitely didn't last that long but Tabby didn't seem to mind. She had found her passion for passion once more and she knew that this was just the beginning, something amazing was just around the corner for her.

She knew that she had something to believe in once more, however sordid, however cheap, however morally abhorrent it may seem to others.

Tabby couldn't say for definite what this wondrous belief in sin, in carnal pleasures would ultimately grant her, but somewhere deep inside, she knew that the key to her happiness would be found.

And she couldn't get the thought of the chapel ruins, on the hill, surrounded by Blackman's Forest, out of her mind.

ALONE

Hugh sat in his Vauxhall Insignia, his hands turning white as he clenched the leather-covered steering-wheel tightly, rocking backwards and forwards in the driver's seat. He muttered incomprehensibly under his breath, grinding his teeth, sweat pouring down the small of his back. The car was filled with the sound of Thrash Metal; the cacophony of roared lyrics, crashing, splintering and soaring electric guitars filling the interior enough to make the windows thrum and vibrate.

Hugh was seething.

He had driven home to Oakleigh from Exeter with the intention of surprising his wife, Dana. He was meant to be on a course for the rest of the week but he'd fallen out with the instructor and had decided to leave, convincing himself that it was a waste of his time and that he should be home with his wife.

Unfortunately Dana had not been home alone when he pulled up outside their terraced house.

Or particularly discreet about being that way.

Dana had always insisted that they kept the curtains pulled after 6pm throughout the year, each and every evening, she liked to have the house well lit inside and didn't want any Tom, Dick or Harriet to be able to see beyond the net curtains when walking past.

Yet as Hugh switched off the car engine and looked up from his driver's seat, he could see as clear as day Dana, standing in the middle of the window. She was bent over the sideboard, lost deep in the throes of passion, still dressed in that god-awful, tattered, old housecoat she loved to wear, being what he could only describe as rutted from behind.

His next door neighbour, Shane, doing the rutting.

Hugh had wanted to leap from the car, smash down the front door and kill the pair of them in a bloody rampage.

But he didn't.

Shane, all 6'4" of muscle-bound Neanderthal, would beat the living shit out of him in the blink of an eye, laughing his head off while he tore him limb from limb and Hugh knew there was not a damn thing he could do about it. He didn't consider himself a coward but there was something about pain that literally scared the shit out of him. He had always turned the other cheek, taken a 'Coward Of The County' stance that had stood him in good stead throughout his thirty-five years on God's green earth.

And watching a solid slab of granite-of-a-man, screwing the arse off of his shapely, gorgeous wife, still wasn't enough for him to become as angry as Bruce Banner and put that theory to the test.

Most people would have turned away,driven away,ran away, closed their eyes even but Hugh just sat there, unable to tear his eyes away, watching this horrendous, heart-stomping, sickening tableau unfold with perfect clarity. Murderous thoughts tore at the fabric of his consciousness, imagining his hands around Dana's throat, imagining driving a ten-inch blade through Shane's sternum, imagining using a shotgun on the pair of them.

The thought of watching them coming and going at

the same time brought a small smile to his flustered, blood-drained face as he watched them throw themselves around the lounge with adulterous abandon, using all manner of surfaces within that room, in their pursuit of sexual nirvana.

Hugh started to think about his own mortality as wave after wave of nausea and despair started to wash over him like a tsunami, the sickening, sinking feeling in the pit of his stomach threatening to send vomit and bile up his throat, the bitter sting of tears pricking his heavy eyes.

He found the lure of suicide raged through his mind as he shivered and shook where he sat. It wasn't the first time in his life that he had seriously contemplated, what most people believed was the coward's way out but catching his wife going at it, with a hulk of a man, gave it maximum shove back into the limelight. Killing them seemed to be no option but killing himself seemed to be easier to think about, which scared him and angered him, in equal measure, making him feel even more nauseous.

How had he let things get to this stage? Had he not been enough for Dana? Was Shane better than him in every way it mattered most?

The questions rifled through his brain in a staccato fashion, almost in time with the steady roar of the music that threatened to drown out each thought, no matter how delirious or delusional.

Then the rage raised its ugly head, snapping him back to reality like the world's biggest rubber band and figuratively slammed him back into the windscreen and back into the car, his eyes upon the fornicating fuckers in his own front room.

He wrung his whitened fingers so hard upon the leather steering-wheel that they threatened to break, imagining once more that he had Dana's throat in his hands, imagining that she was choking on something rather than what Shane was giving her.

He looked back at the window of his house and saw

Dana, standing splayed against the window, her eyes shut tight, laughing and obviously crying out, the man-mountain stood behind her, his hands on top of her hands, the net-curtains failing to hide either of their modesties.

Something snapped in Hugh and his scream of frustration, fury and pure rage drowned out the Thrash Metal music and rocked the car, if not the street itself, birds would have flown from the wires, cats would have screeched and run in all directions.

But his wife and her lover failed to notice, or more accurately, heard his cries of anguish. They were at it as Hugh clambered out of his car and strode angrily across the dimly-lit street. Shane was still ploughing Dana as if his life depended on it when Hugh threw the door open.

The first time Shane realised that the man of the house had returned was when Hugh cracked him hard across the back of the head with Hugh's cricket bat that he had picked up from his sports-bag inside the front door. Shane slumped to the floor, blood gushing from the back of his head, his eyes rolled back.

Dana, still gasping and groaning as if she was having an asthma attack, her dishevelled robe barely covering what was left of her diminished modesty threatening to slip from her bare shoulders, finally turned and screamed.

Hugh was stood over her unconscious, prone lover, breathing heavy, his face a pale mask of furious anger, the bloody cricket-bat clenched like a vice in both fists, his eyes upon her.

"What have you done?" she screamed, desperately trying to pull her robe together, the flimsy one-piece she wore beneath twisted and cutting into her bared chest.

"What have I done?" Hugh laughed incredulously, letting his left hand fall away from the handle of the bat, "i catch you fucking this dickhead and you ask 'what have I done'?"

"You've killed him!" Dana shrieked, sinking to her knees, her modesty no longer covered by robe or slip as she knelt beside Shane.

"The bastard will wake up with a fucker of a headache but no, he's not dead."

Dana started to cry, tears streaming down her make-up stained face, her hands upon Shane's pallid face.

"Though you may be."

Hugh raised the bat above his head with one hand, his eyes on the side of Dana's head, knowing where he wanted to bring the bat crashing down.

Instead, he was doubling over as Dana balled up her fist and punched him square in the crotch, white hot pain erupting between his legs, his scream of agony louder than any he had already released that evening in the car. He was on his knees, coughing and spluttering, clutching his aching testicles as if his life depended on it, rocking on his haunches.

Dana, breasts exposed, her perspiration-covered body glistening in the light of the transparent lampshade overhead, reached for the fallen bat and without saying a word, cracked him upon the side of his head.

The world went dark as all Hugh could think was how much his balls hurt, much, much more than his heart which she had snapped in two.

Hugh's eyes flicked open tentatively, bright sunlight filtering through his eyelids before they opened fully. As the world swam into view, the pain inside his cranium exploded as bright as a million suns his hand went to his thundering temple, his head suddenly feeling heavier than humanly possible.

He was laying face down upon his living room carpet, a small pool of his own blood soaked into the beige fibres, his balls aching as if a herd of elephants had decided to traipse over his groin on their daily parade. He was alone in the lounge, no sign of Dana and her dickhead, the room bathed in what appeared to be morning sunlight, the sunlight cascading through the very window where he had witnessed his wife's betrayal. The net-curtain was lopsided and pulled to one side where she had held on for dear life and Hugh could see handprints smeared in the dust, as well as what appeared to be her lips and possibly her boobs too.

He knew she wasn't particularly house-proud but he supposed her dusting and window-cleaning was the least of his problems now and writhing around with her extremities jiggling around and smeared in the window indicated thusly.

The pounding in his head was at least drowning out the dull ache in his balls as he dragged himself to his feet and held on to dear life to the back of the sofa. The room swam a little until he managed to get his bearings and stand unaided, if not a little unsure, on his feet.

Glancing slowly at his watch, as quick movements were definitely not advisable while a marching band kept its own beat in his head.

Bon Jovi slipping into his thoughts was certainly not helping, however prophetic and apt their lyrics seemed to be.

It was roughly 10am which meant he had been out for the count for nearly 12 hours and he winced at the thought of her knock-out blow once more, its reverberation powering through his mind once again.

The house was deathly quiet, not a creak of the old floorboards, not a soft breeze rattling a door or window, no footsteps in the rooms above.

Hugh thought that if there was a breeze a tumble-weed would idle by like it was some old Western frontier town.

That made him smile.

Then he realised that Dana had probably made a swift exit from the family home, probably stopping to aim a swift kick to his head while he was counting sheep, before spitting on him, stepping over him then leaving with that overgrown, ignorant, muscle-head.

ALONE

There seemed to be nothing missing from the living room but he didn't expect her to take the various pictures of the pair of them that they had accumulated throughout their five year marriage, no matter how good she looked in them. She always did look pretty stunning in a bikini but she could wear a black, bin-bag and still look like she had stepped off a catwalk or from the pages of Hello magazine; her favourite fantasy.

Yet the pics of them in Las Vegas, at The Grand Canyon, The Seychelles, New York and The Maldives all remained, pride of place upon the walls of their tastefully decorated lounge.

Her Jackie Collins, Harold Robbins and Jilly Cooper hardback books still sat upon the dusty shelves, her Robbie Williams, Michael Buble and Beyoncé C. CDs remained in their shelving unit, her garish, yet vacuous and inane magazines lay upon the coffee table, as if they lived in some crummy dentist's waiting room.

Hugh stumbled up the open-plan staircase, steadying himself upon the wrought-iron bannister rail as his feet just about managed to take a step at a time.

Stepping into the bedroom, he could see that the bed hadn't been slept in for a while, not that it surprised him in the slightest, judging on last nights revelation. What did surprise him though was that the wardrobe was still full of her clothes, her blouses, her skirts, her suits still hanging in perfect, regimented order as she liked to keep them. Her rows upon rows of superfluous footwear lay untouched in the shoe-rack beside the wardrobe. Her underwear, some sexy, but mostly practical and plain, still lay in her sweetly-scented drawers and he saw her tattered, old housecoat and singlet laying upon the bed, almost as if she had faded away while still wearing them.

Their suitcases still sat in the spare bedroom, untouched and still empty, as were her couple of sports-holdalls that she sometimes used when they went away for a weekend.

He then caught sight of outside and ran, or more accurately, fell down the staircase and threw open the front door.

Dana's white Vauxhall Astra was parked directly outside the house, right in front of the black Ford Focus RS that Shaun-The-Prick liked to drive like some oversized 'boy-racer' despite being in his 40's.

'That must be it' Hugh thought to himself, with an apathetic shrug of his shoulders.

Dana, sweet acrobatic, supple Dana who finally found her sexual adventurism while swinging off the chandelier, figuratively speaking, must have gone next door with the Neanderthal.

Hugh considered for a second, the idea that he should knock on the door and tell the dickhead that he was welcome to her but that evaporated quite quickly when he remembered how big the motherfucker was and more importantly, how Hugh had knocked him out the night before.

As he stood there, he half-expected the bastard's front door to fly open and him to come flying at Hugh, ripping Hugh's head off his shoulders as easy as pulling the wings off a fly.

But nothing happened.

Hugh, with dried blood caked on the side of his face, his crumpled suit resembling being slept in, his balls and his brain aching like complete bastards as he squinted in the morning sun, realised that the street was complete deserted. There was no sound of birds up on the wires or in the trees that lined the avenue, there was no children playing, no mothers reprimanding them for playing, no cars, lorries or vehicles of any kind thundering past his door like they did nearly every other morning.

Hugh did consider the fact that the blow from Dana had rendered him stone deaf but even if that was so, there was nothing moving in his street, nothing at all.

At the opposite end of his street, nearly two hundred

yards away, he could just about make out Oakleigh's Main Street but nothing seemed to be moving there either. He looked up to the heavens, looking for plane trails overhead, hoping to see those goddamn birds flying in the cloudy, yet sunny summer sky overhead.

Nothing.

He checked his watch and saw that the hands hadn't moved and shaking it comically as if in some silly cartoon would make it work suddenly.

It didn't.

He gulped for a shot of courage and walked to Shane's front-door, rapping loudly upon the black door.

'In for a penny, in for a pound' he thought, standing nervously upon his neighbour's doorstep, knowing that if the door did indeed open, his feet wouldn't touch the ground as Shane's uppercut would send him sprawling.

There was no answer.

Hugh then contemplated kicking in the door, if he was going to get his arse handed to him then he ought to make some collateral damage of his own and an inanimate door was a good start.

But instead, he turned the handle, pushing the door open gently.

The laminate-floored hallway of Shane's house was a little dark and dingy but Hugh stepped over the threshold and inside. He thought about calling out but if he didn't have to alert Shane to his presence, it would probably turn out for the best. He also ran the risk that he'd catch them in a compromising situation once more but as far as he was concerned, that horse had bolted, that cat was out of the bag, that bird had flown the coop.

And with a gnawing realisation nibbling at the back of his mind, Hugh decided, once again, that it was the least of his problems.

He was pleasantly but of course, grudgingly surprised that Shane's house seemed quite tasteful and not the macho, lager-lout, man-cave that he had expected.

Naturally there was a plethora of weight-lifting equipment in the lounge and walk-through dining area but the house seemed to be decorated with a lot of pastel shades, soft furnishings and even flowers in vases upon sideboards and tables.

Hugh then realised that he was probably receiving 'a woman's touch' a little too close to Hugh's home for comfort.

But Shane's house was equally quiet and equally empty as Hugh's had been.

Hugh stumbled back outside, deciding against exploring his neighbour's house further, slightly afraid he'd find more clues that his wife had been jumping Shane's bones in his home, probably her sexiest underwear or heaven-forbid, her 'sexy nurse's' outfit draped upon what would no doubt be black, silk sheets upon Shane's bed.

He stood back out in the street, cocking his head to one side like an intelligent Collie dog, listening hard for any sound that might tell him that he wasn't going crazy. He'd take deafness any day of the week as long as he knew there was something happening, as long as he knew that there wasn't something wrong in his world, something wrong in Oakleigh.

Hugh walked to his Insignia, noticing he had left his keys in the car's ignition in his haste to confront his wanton wife and her violent lover.

He sat in the driver's seat and turned the key.

There came a clunk from the column but the car failed to turn over, the lights were on the dashboard but the engine had failed to spark.

With the noise from the steering column, he realised his hearing was fine and his internal ear hadn't been doing all the work. He banged his fists on the plastic dash to confirm this and almost sighed with relief.

But that didn't explain why his car hadn't started.

He supposed that the battery could have drained since he'd been sat in it last but the light for the RDS radio was still on. He pressed the play button for the CD and the Thrash metal blared from the speakers, deafening him once again. Hugh pressed the button for the FM radio but only static filled the car, he tried each and every radio station stored in the player but each was the same.

Nothing but static.

Hugh slunk from the car, his aches intensifying as he stood erect and squinting, he looked at the sky once more.

He wasn't sure how much time had passed but it seemed to him that the sun had remained in the same position as it had earlier.

Then, from far away, Hugh could hear the very faint sound of music playing, turning his head, he surmised that it was coming from the town and set off in that direction.

Within his immediate vicinity, he could only hear his footfalls upon the pavement as he walked down the street, his eyes darting from side to side, in each house's windows as he walked past.

Each house was seemingly deserted.

Hugh quickened his pace as he reached the corner of Main Street, yet the sound of music had seemed to have stayed the same distance away from him.

Main Street, Oakleigh's main thoroughfare was full of cars, some parked askew, some parked normally but each shop, each building, each hairdresser's, charity shop and boutique store was completely quiet and deserted.

Hugh was beginning to panic at the absurdity of it all.

Oakleigh was a ghost town.

And the music, still faint, coming from past Upper Bridge Street that lead up out of the town, played on.

Hugh thought he recognised the music but it was far enough away to sound like the tinny music you heard when someone was listening to a Walkmans headphones, back in the 80's.

Walking up towards Upper Bridge Street, towards the river bridge and the lanes beyond reminded Hugh of those long walks home when he was a child, those quiet, lonely walks when the world was asleep, sometime before dawn when he'd walk his paper-round. He used to love that time of the day when it seemed he was the only person in the world, revelling in the solitude and silence.

As an adult, during the day, this was not as magical and charming.

It was downright terrifying.

Crossing the old bridge that straddled the town's river, Hugh looked back down at Oakleigh nestling in the bottom of that valley, his home town that lay like a small, yet sprawling cemetery and just as deathly silent.

And the music played on.

Now though, it sounded a little louder, coming from the direction of Blackman Forest, the thickly wooded copse that ringed Richards Hill, the forest that encased the chapel ruins upon it's peak.

Hugh used to go up there when he was a kid, ignoring the rumours that it was a haunted place, ignoring people when he was told that dead bodies had been found up there, ignoring the rumours that men and women used to worship the devil within the hallowed ground. He had never found anything untoward up there as a child and the place had lost his lustre when he became a man, though he wasn't surprised that illicit couples used to frequent the area for their 'romantic' trysts.

He found himself wondering if Dana and Shane had ever parked up in the small car-park he found himself walking through at that precise time, wondered if they had walked up the same shaded woodland path that led to the top of the hill.

He bet they hadn't followed the sound of what suspiciously sounded like Led Zeppelin's 'Stairway To Heaven' emanating from up ahead.

Hugh's heavy footfalls were loud in the shrouded path, fallen branches, twigs and leaves all crunching underfoot as he stumbled upwards, following the curve of the path and the hill to where he knew the ruins of the small chapel lay waiting.

Along with whoever was playing that seminal 70's rock classic on a continuous loop, its soft acoustic guitar accompaniment giving way to thumping drums and scathing electric guitar salvoes time after time.

Hugh rounded the top of the hill, the wind rifling through the canopy of the trees as he stepped reticently into the clearing, the small, ham-stone ruins of the chapel sitting dappled in the unmoving sunlight directly overhead.

There, against the crumbling, decimated north wall of the chapel, covered with ivy and vines that snaked across its bricks like lines on a map, leant a man.

The man was easily 6'4" tall and seemingly as wide and for an instant Hugh though it was Shane, Shane who had fucked his wife and was now waiting to fuck Hugh up.

But the man had flowing blonde hair that came down past his backside, a knee-length blonde beard and seemed to be wearing a white suit that was as dazzling as that blazing sun in the sky.

The man reminded Hugh of what he perceived as a Viking with the flowing mane, the flowing beard and the bluest eyes he had ever seen on a man and more worryingly, a double-bladed axe propped against the broken wall.

"Ah Hugh," the man's voice boomed through the clearing, making Hugh's ears ring, "you finally made it! Good!"

The music stopped instantly.

As did the wind through the trees.

And seemingly Hugh's breathing and heartbeat.

"What's happening?" Hugh stammered, suddenly wishing that he hadn't driven back from Exeter yesterday, let alone walked up that fucking hill, "why am I here?"

The tall blonde man picked up the axe and tossed it up like it was as light as a feather, the shimmering blade reflecting the sunlight as it arced through the air before the man deftly caught it in the other. It reminded Hugh of

Chris Hemsworth's portrayal and hammer-juggling scene in Thor. Though Hugh somehow knew this wasn't for laughs.

Or a cinematic throwaway.

"Do you know where you are?" the man asked, juggling the long axe from hand to hand as he started walking around the perimeter of the crumbled ruins, "do you know what this place is?"

Hugh wondered if this was a series of trick questions, maybe a test to ascertain his own sanity and lucidity.

The man seemed to read his mind.

"This is no test Hugh," the man sighed, seemingly attempting to avoid his gaze, "that wasn't a trick question. More of a rhetorical one, if I'm honest."

Hugh started to back away from the clearing but as the man brought his steely gaze to bear upon him, those piercingly-blue eyes fixing him with a look of both contempt and daring, in equal measure.

"This place is Death. This unholy, desecrated place is testament to the evil that has blighted this town for hundreds of years."

"Where has everyone gone?"

Hugh stood still, his departure from that place halted by the man's obvious disapproving glare, now standing looking at the behemoth of a man with the beautiful, yet scary axe, knowing there was nowhere for him to go.

" To steal Stephen King's parlance from The Dark Tower, 'the world has moved on' Hugh," the man laughed, his booming laughter shaking the very trees that surrounded the clearing, "though technically for you it hasn't my dear fellow. It's just taken a side step. You have slipped into what I'd like to call 'the periphery', almost between two worlds if you like."

Hugh was confused to the point that his head ached from trying to think about it, more than the knock-out blow that Dana had delivered.

"You're dead, me ol' China," he continued, "Dana

staved your head in good and proper Hugh, blood and brains everywhere. Looked like a Peckinpah movie."

Hugh's mouth fell open almost comically that he could almost hear the sound-effect of something falling, rattling around in the back of his head.

"You ought to see your face," the man giggled like a teenager, "mind you, most make that face when I tell them they're dead, then comes the crying, the wailing, the gnashing of teeth, the pleading for forgiveness."

"So who are you?" Hugh said quietly, still struggling to understand what the hell was going on, the surreal words of the tall, long-haired, long-bearded, blonde man failing to get through his befuddled thoughts.

The man started walking in Hugh's direction, the grass, the crumbled masonry, the leaves and the moss barely moving with each earth-trembling step. Hugh could feel the ground shake from within but where he stood he could see no change in the surroundings.

"I have no name," the man said, the deepness of his voice, though smooth like aural caramel, adding gravitas to his words, "but I suppose your kind would call me some kind of 'headhunter', to use your vernacular."

Hugh's confusion didn't seem to be abating any time soon.

"I collect souls, a person's soul to be precise. And I have to take their heads in order to collect their soul."

Hugh's eyes were upon the twirling, undulating, juggled axe that went from large hand to large hand.

"A little barbaric, I'll grant you but very effective nonetheless."

"Is this Purgatory?" Hugh stammered, watching the huge man step ever closer, "am I destined for Heaven or Hell?"

The man stopped in his tracks and stood blinking like a deer stuck in dazzling headlights, a look of bemusement spreading across his bearded face.

"My dear Hugh...there is no Heaven or Hell, there is

no God or Devil, no angels or demons. There will be no bargain, no deal, no damnation or salvation. I take your soul, that's it."

It was Hugh's turn to look like the deer caught in high-beams, though there was no bemusement upon his face, just bewilderment and terror.

"You come from darkness, you're thrust into this life and you go out in darkness, that's that. No do-overs, no miraculous come-backs, finito!"

"You said that I've slipped into the periphery, almost like being stuck in two worlds," Hugh stammered, the words tripping over, rather than off his tongue, "so what is the second world?"

"There is no second world, meat-sack!" the man bellowed and this time the earth did shake beneath his feet, fresh leaves falling from the trees around the clearing, "there is nothing but darkness outside of here, nothing but darkness!"

The large man stopped juggling the axe and glared menacingly at Hugh, seemingly flexing his entire massive frame, muscle upon muscle rippling beneath his Italian-cut, single-breasted suit.

"Surely there is something I can do?" Hugh pleaded, sinking slowly to his knees upon the dry undergrowth, the branches and lichen crackling beneath his knees, "I'm a good man, I've led a good life."

"Good has got nothing to do with it." the man growled, "you are dead Hugh, as the proverbial door nail and I am taking your head."

Hugh watched the man get closer and closer, hopelessness and despair washing over him in a tidal wave that dwarfed the one he felt the night before while watching Dana, being spread-eagled, across the living room window, for the world to see.

"It's not fair!" Hugh wailed, tears beginning to roll down his burning cheeks, "it's not fair. Dana cheated on me. Dana fucking killed me! She should be here, not me, it's not fucking fair!"

The axe-wielding man, with it raised above his head, about to deliver the closest and most final shave that Hugh would ever have, stopped.

"Whoever said any of this was fair?" he laughed, "or made any sense whatsoever?"

Hugh screamed as the axe whistled through the air in a downwards motion, his executioner's laughter echoing around the wooded clearing.

Then there was nothing.

Until Hugh's eyes flicked open and he found himself in his Insignia, driving back to Oakleigh on the Exeter road, dusk beginning to fall around the picturesque South West countryside.

The scream died on his lips as the sound of Slipknot filled the car's interior, the steering getting away from him for a split second but he managed to realign the wheels to stop him careering into the hedgerow.

His mind was beginning to lose its lucidity, the thoughts quickly turning to swirling, misty fragments that he grasped at to keep them in reach but they were starting to get away from him.

He could just about remember watching Dana being ravaged by an unknown, yet massive man, while he sat in his car. He could remember 'Stairway To Heaven' being played in a wooded area. He could remember Chris Hemsworth.

He could remember a double-bladed axe.

But by the time his Insignia thudded over South Bridge Road's bridge, entering the outskirts of Oakleigh, the only thing Hugh was sure of was that he shouldn't go home quite yet, the wispy fragments of memories disappearing into the recesses of his mind.

Something was telling him that instead of going home, he should go to The Griffon pub for a quick drink.

Something was telling him to call Dana to let her

know he was back home in Oakleigh, to see if she wanted him to pick up a Chinese takeaway and a bottle of wine.

Something was telling him that he ought to sit down with his wife and have a heart-to-heart.

Something was telling him that there was something seriously wrong with their marriage and if they didn't discuss these fears, then he was sure they wouldn't survive.

It was almost like his life depended on it.

FROM THE INSIDE

"I'm leaving you."

The second I heard myself say those words, I knew instantly that life would never, ever be the same again.

I watched his face crumple and thought that he would burst into tears there and then but he looked up from his Kindle with a look of resignation etched upon his hairy face, his brown eyes looking directly into mine.

I wanted to crumple myself.

Instead, I offered a weak smile, trying my hardest to let him know that I was OK, trying to make him believe that I was strong, that I could do this.

I wasn't sure if it was him, or myself, that I was trying to convince.

I was standing in front of our glorious bay window that overlooked the driveway, feeling the hot sun burning on my neck, hoping that the sun's rays cascading through hadn't turned my floral, summer dress transparent.

Not that Joe would notice.

I was smiling at him, a weak smile that belied my true feelings, my true intentions. I guessed he'd probably think I was mocking him, probably think I was leering at him, lording over him.

But my heart was breaking.

Joe had, what I would call, a 'skew-whiff' slant on the world, his depression and anxiety making him see, think, hear and god knows, even taste things differently. It wasn't his fault per Se, it was that god-damn affliction that changed everything about him., who he was, what he was, who he had become.

So my smile, as small and unobtrusive as I was trying to make it, was probably being interpreted as me mocking him.

I had to look away.

For months, I'd had to watch him sit on that frigging sofa, his eyes glued to that god-damn e-book, reading his Stephen King, 'weird shit'. He was no doubt trying to escape in to whatever strange world was hidden within those words and electronic pages. Because he sure-as-shit wasn't spending any time, or effort, in the real world with me.

He hadn't shaved in weeks, hadn't cut his hair in months and was beginning to look like some tramp that had walked in off the streets, some vagabond that would beg on street corners for change.

But that didn't bother me in the slightest.

I didn't care that he wasn't clean shaven or clean cut, I was never hung up on how he presented himself, unless we were going out obviously. I did like the look of him when he kept his hair short, mainly because I have always had a thing for cropped hair, especially if his beard stubble was kept to a minimum.

My family were always going on at me at how Joe looked like a slob, how he lounged around the house all day, doing absolutely fuck all. Always moaning that all he wore was shorts and t-shirts each and every day. Moaned that he smoked like a chimney and yet never paid for his cigarettes.

But they had no idea what he was going through, no idea and didn't really give a shit anyway. They thought he was just lazy, just an attention-seeker, just a waste of space.

But I knew different.

I knew how his mental health was killing him by degrees.

I knew that unless I did something, he would waste away before my very eyes and I had tried so many different ways to help. I had cajoled him, encouraged him, supported him, mothered him even but all to no avail.

So OK, telling him I was leaving him was probably not the greatest way to go about it, I never said my plan would be perfect did I?

I never told him where I was going.

Never told him that I was going to stay away completely.

I just wanted to shock him into doing something.

But there had been nothing; no begging or pleading me not to go, no anger that I was going to walk out on him, nothing to show me that I was making a big mistake.

Of course, throughout our years of marriage, we'd had good times, bad times, even indifferent times but this was possibly the worst I had ever known it.

Worse than when he cheated on me.

Worse than when he left me.

Worse than when he tried to kill himself.

He'd been a dick more times than I'd care to mention but I still loved the very bones of him, loved him to the moon and back and for ever and a day.

Even though he was and always would be, a dick.

I had always been brought up to believe in the sanctity of marriage, to believe that if something was broken, you didn't throw it away.

You bloody fixed it!

Or at least tried to.

But, and it was a BIG but, there is always only so much you can do, only so much you can do before you give up banging your head against a mad bugger's wall.

Yeah, I listened to his Pink Floyd depressing shite.

Spending 20 years with a geeky, introverted, pop-culture loving, man-child, I was bound to pick up some of his nuances, some of his more obscure references, some of his weird and wonderful tidbits.

And the fucker always made me laugh.

But I wasn't laughing now.

Not inside and definitely not outwardly.

I'm pretty sure Joe had some weird ideas about how I thought every now and again, pretty sure that he thought I was stronger than I actually was.

I was strong when I was younger, long before life had decided to take a huge dump on me, a huge dump from a great height that covered me from head to toe. I fought tooth and nail for every inch that life afforded me, fought like a lioness protecting her cubs.

But even a lioness gets tired, gets worn down, can't provide for the pride any longer if the pickings are slim around the savannah.

And Joe, sure as eggs is eggs, ain't no Mufasa, or Simba at a push.

But I'm rambling.

I walked toward the front door, picking up the holdall I had prepared that very morning, my floppy sandals clacking noisily upon the laminated floor in the hallway.

I was waiting for Joe to shout after me, waiting for Joe to beg and plead for me not to walk out the door, waiting for him to say 'stop, in the name of love.'

But there was nothing.

No shouting, no gnashing of teeth, no begging, no pleading, nothing.

With trembling hand, I opened the heavy, wooden door, the blinding sunlight flooding through the doorway as I stepped over the threshold. I even hesitated slightly, my fingers around the door handle, hanging on to the last vestiges of my marriage by my chipped, bitten and faded fingernails, praying that he would call after me, come running after me.

He didn't.

My head started to ache, the blazing sun made me squint badly and I instantly regretted not picking up my Gucci sunglasses from the kitchen table. I was damned if I was going to walk back inside though.

Even though I really, really wanted to.

Even though it was stifling hot today, there was a slight breeze so I was glad that I had chosen to wear my favourite summer dress, the gentle wind tickled my long, brown hair around my face and gave me a thin coating of goosebumps upon my bare arms.

My feet crunched the gravel of the driveway underfoot as I made my way to my black BMW, the sound of the birds up on the wires and in the trees heralding my departure like a guard of honour. There were kids outside in the street, enjoying their summer holidays, whooping and hollering as if to tell the world I was walking out on my husband.

Walking out on my home, on my marriage, my depressed and possibly suicidal man.

But I wasn't really.

My intention was to shock the bastard into fighting for me, shock him into taking stock of his life, our marriage even and to fight for it all.

To fight for me.

I had always been the one to try and make this all work, always the one to fight for everything, always the one to be the voice of reason. That wasn't to say I did everything, that he did absolutely nothing. For years we had been a team, a union that stood together under some of the worst scrutiny and worst trials and tribulations that would have fucked anyone over. We had traversed treacherous, choppy waters that battered the 'good ship Mr & Mrs Fender' upon an evil sea that would have sunk any other couple and we had come through the other side upon a brave, new world.

We had always said it had been the two of us against

the world, two of us facing whatever this shitty life threw at us and keeping strong, keeping together.

But it had all been in vain.

All been a big lie.

All wrong.

Joe had been carrying this god-damn disease deep inside him, this debilitating illness that made him a liar, a malaise that made him question each and every aspect of himself, his world, his life. It had been there all the time, festering beneath the surface, chipping away at the facade he had apparently erected around himself, ever since he was a young boy. There had always been a sombre side to him, a melancholy that reared its head every now and again but he had hidden it well, had made everyone believe that he was functioning normally.

But depression was killing him, inch by inch, minute by minute, year by year.

There had been episodes over the years, some slight, some severe but he had battled through, with my help, his family's help, his friends help until now.

Joe had closed out everyone who he held dear, made that stupid fucking wall so high that nothing and no one could penetrate and even though we battered it as much as humanly possible each and every day, it wasn't even making a scratch. He'd gone so far inside himself that he threatened to disappear up his own arsehole in a puff of smoke, not the nicest image I'm sure you'd agree.

Family, friends and even strangers had tried their damnedest to help him, to talk to him, recommended therapists to him, recommended therapy to get him through all this.

But he stuck his head in the sand yet again, tried his hardest to block it all out, buried his head, figuratively, into that damned, fucking Kindle of his.

Part of me found myself wondering if he somehow revelled in it all, wondering if he found solace in the darkness that clawed at him from deep within his own mind.

Did he like being that way?

Did he want to be depressed because, though it was a nasty fucking way to live, it was easier for him?

I tried my best not to think that way, tried not to believe that for all the darkness that enveloped him, it was easier than living a normal, healthy life, a life that would ultimately make him happy and content.

I had to believe that he wanted to live.

Of course, I wanted it to be with me.

Always had been, always would.

But I found it so damn hard to watch him self-implode, to watch him struggle to pull himself out of bed every fucking morning.

Was my leaving going to make him realise what he was losing by following such a dark, dangerous path, by giving up on life, by pushing me away more than anyone else?

Some would judge me, some would believe that I didn't care about him, no doubt there would be hints and allegations, lies and deceit, the rumour mill of Oakleigh would no doubt start working overtime. I suppose its the same in each and every town, small communities mean small-minded idiots with too much interest in the lives of others, rather than concentrating on their own petty, insignificant lives.

To quote REO Speedwagon "the talk is cheap when the story is good and the tales grow taller on down the line."

Especially is this shitty, little town.

Still, least it wasn't Chard.

Now THAT was a town full of small-minded, opinionated, small-town mentality with a snarling, drooling, teeth-baring contempt for human life and an unhealthy interest in everyone else's lives with no regard for their own. Everyone knew every aspect of everyone's lives there, the gossips would have a field day with the story of a hard-working and loving wife that left her depressed husband to fend for himself.

No doubt it would have gone around like wildfire that I had shacked up with his best mate, probably been shagging him for months behind my husband's back.

OK, I'd be the first to admit that I had talked to Colin, at great length, but really just about Joe. Yes, he was a charismatic, handsome guy who had an eye for the ladies and a sweet word that seemed to be able to charm the knickers off any female that gave him the eye.

But I'd never cheated on Joe in all the years we had been together, even though I was a hot-blooded woman who had needs, a woman who had yearnings that needed sating, just like anyone else.

Colin never came on to me, just offered a friendly ear to bend, an opinion if ever asked for, a warm, caring shoulder to cry on. We'd met for coffee now and again, even bumped into each other on a booze-fuelled night out but nothing sexual ever happened.

Yeah, I can her you now, 'so says you.'

But it's the truth.

OK, so its flattering to be wanted by another man, to be desired, to be lusted after but Colin was not like that, no one had been like that and I swear I wasn't interested in another man.

I wanted Joe.

I loved Joe.

He may paint me like some scarlet woman in the future, may lash out towards me and all I am, may think I'm a hard-hearted, cold woman that has taken his heart and stomped all over it with my dainty little feet.

That was not my intention.

That is not who I am.

I have no ulterior motive, no master-plan, no great design.

I'm just a woman who has no idea how to get the man I love to love his life again, to be the man I know he can be, to become the man I fell in love with all those years ago.

I don't want to change him, want him to be something he's not, want to tear him apart and start all over again.

I just want him to be happy.

I started the car's engine and took a last look at the living-room window in my rear-view mirror. I was hoping and praying that he would appear in the bay window, hoping he would pound on the glass and dramatically scream out loud, scream for me not to go.

He didn't.

With tears stinging my eyes, I pulled slowly out of the driveway, dragging out the moment of departure as much as I could without stalling the BMW, or flattening the children out playing in the street. A couple of them waved and I feebly returned the favour, feeling the corners of my mouth turning down, their glowing, cheery little faces failing to put a smile on my own.

Bruno Mars was extolling the virtues of 'Uptown Funk' from my car's CD player, his gloriously sexy voice filling the car.

I switched it off instantly.

I didn't feel like being in a dancing mood, didn't feel like Bruno was the appropriate voice to be swimming around inside my head for the next few hours, no matter how smooth the fucker was.

I must admit, some of Joe's current music was a little dark and heavy, he seemed to have a fascination with Corey Taylor at the moment, whether it was his solo career, Stone Sour or heaven forbid, fucking Slipknot. Their song 'Snuff' seemed to be on repeat, which I found a little disconcerting and possibly was truly expressing how he felt about me but I hoped not. I knew that he did consider himself 'too dark to care', did think that I 'couldn't hate enough to love' but I hoped and prayed that he didn't think I had sold him out to save myself.

That's not what any of this was about, none of it.

I loved him with all my heart, all my body, all my soul, that had never changed through all the shit that was happening in our lives, had never changed in all the years we had been together.

I had no idea where I was driving to as I headed toward Oakleigh town centre, the car driving at what seemed like a snail's pace through the sun-dappled, pedestrian-heavy streets. Cars, lorries, motorbike and bicycles clogging up the roads like normal which I always found as fascinating as annoying for such a small, hokey little town. I drove toward Main Street, watching the townsfolk going around their business seemingly without a care in the world, laughing, chatting, living their own little lives, without any regard for the torment I was going through.

My heart was breaking as I watched the world going by, seemingly turning while I was figuratively standing still, my life in perpetual limbo. Each breath, measured yet erratic, took me further away from the man I loved when all I wanted to do was be there for him, to live my life with him, to be the woman he wanted above all else.

A few times I felt like slamming my foot upon the accelerator and send my car smashing into the nearest lamp-post, crumpling the car with myself in it into a brick wall.

But I didn't.

I wanted to be strong, wanted to be the woman I used to be, wanted to show myself that leaving Joe, however gut-wrenching, however soul-destroying, was for the greater good.

And smashing myself to pieces in this German engineering wasn't going to do that.

And in all honesty, the air-bags would put paid to that anyway.

And all it would have done was shown that BMW

drivers really were the arrogant, self-centred dickheads they were normally portrayed as. And Christ knows I've had that accusation thrown my way since I bought the fucking thing.

I found myself driving up out of the town, Upper Bridge Street leading me over the northern bridge that lay on the outskirts of Oakleigh, the road out of the town that led off towards Chard, Ilminster and beyond.

But I screeched around a sharp bend, sliding the car expertly into an off-shooting country lane that diverted me off the course out of the town.

I was going toward Blackman Forest.

I had decided that I was going to park up and take a breather in that small car-park, near the wood, the wood that encircled Richard's Hill and the chapel ruins. I knew I would be able to see Oakleigh laid out before me, to see my home town in all its resplendent glory, the place where Joe and I had spent our lives together, leading to this very moment.

The car-park was deserted, luckily those supposed cheating couples that frequented this place didn't spend much time up here during the day. I did consider getting out of the car and taking the quick walk up that little, sheltered, woodland path that led up to the hidden ruins but in all honesty, that place gave me the fucking creeps. Joe had told me that there was an old town rumour that those ruins were haunted and that a witch was burned alive up there hundreds of years ago.

I had heard that the same dogging couples that used this actual car-park after dark were the only moans and groans heard up by the chapel ruins, apparently the 'Hanging Tree' was large enough to accommodate more than a couple 'patrons' of a night time.

Joe and I had been quite adventurous once upon a time but neither of us would ever come to this place for bit of 'hanky-panky', both of us had just a little bit of humility and self-esteem.

Over the years we'd dressed up for each other, done a bit of role-play now and again, hell, there was even an old, VHS tape of the two of us somewhere when we were young, foolish and a little more slender than we are now.

But even we would draw the line at coming to Richard's Hill for a fuck.

I pressed the window button and left it fully open before turning off the car's engine, listening to the birds in the trees singing their fucking heads off like it was the bloody dawn chorus.

It was lunchtime.

I could just about hear the rumble of the traffic down in the town as well as the rolling river bubbling beneath the old stone bridge at the north of the town. I could see Main Street, bisecting the town as it snaked through the middle of it all and the lower bridge that stood at the lowest point of Oakleigh. I could just about make out the large trading estate which housed Oakleigh Comprehensive on the outskirts of the town.

What I would give to be back there, to be a fifteen year old girl back there without a care in the word, surrounded by like-minded, empty sponges with hopes and dreams unfulfilled or realised. If I knew back then what I knew now I would have clung onto my school days like a vice and made sure I truly made sure that they were the best days of my life.

I found myself remembering a young boy, I used to know, Charlie Ingram. We used to meet every morning, every lunch-time, sitting in the corridor between our classrooms and talk about absolutely every thing. Both of us mad on Bon Jovi, Byker Grove and Smash Hits, putting the world to rights each and every day, laughing, joking, sharing sweets like nobodies business.

I smiled to myself at the memory then felt it slip as I remembered what had happened to him.

Charlie had enlisted in the army, in the infantry and gone off to fight for his country.

And died back in 1991, been killed by a landmine outside Basra.

Looking at Oakleigh, I momentarily forgot about all my troubles and just took in the glorious, picturesque countryside of this fantastic corner of South Somerset. People used to moan about the towns in the area but there was no denying that this was a beautiful part of the West Country. There were fields of gold and green as far as the eye could see, winding country lanes that were a joy to walk up and down, rivers, crumbling, old bridges, deserted old train tracks, numbers of WW2 pillboxes scattered around the countryside.

Luckily Chard and Ilminster were the other side of the hill so they didn't blight the landscape I was currently gazing at but like most places, from a distance, they were just as pretty to look upon.

But Oakleigh, strange, quirky, funny little Oakleigh with its hauntings, its aged buildings, its ancient bridges, its ruined chapel upon the hill was my home town and I was damn sure that I would never leave.

As much as I would never truly leave Joe.

My thoughts went back to him as I heard sirens drifting up from the centre of the town, seeing the flashing of blue lights snaking up from the direction of Oakleigh police station and the community hospital.

I hoped to god that it was nothing to do with him, hoped and prayed that he hadn't done something REALLY stupid. Hoped that there was just an accident in the town centre. Hoped he hadn't thought our lives together were over and that he had to do something to ease his pain.

I pulled my iPhone from my handbag and scrolled through my contacts, his name appearing upon the screen.

I put the phone to my ear, listening to the ringing from the other end, urging him to pick up, wanting to desperately hear his soft-spoken voice on the end of the line.

I think I will always be waiting to hear his voice again.

Same as i always wake up in the middle of the night, drenched in sweat, screaming his name, clinging to the remnants of a dream where he picks up the phone, tells me he loves me and for me to come home.

I miss him.

'TIS THE SEASON

Rebekah instantly regretted stepping outside her office building's door, the wind buffeting her, the snow flurries blinding her, making her catch her breath.

The storm had been raging for hours, snow falling with such ferocity that there was a real danger that Oakleigh would become cut off from the outside world. The two bridges that stood at opposite sides of the town, the only way in and out of Oakleigh were already crumbling into disrepair, any more snow and there was a distinct possibility they could give way.

And living on the wrong side of the southern bridge, that meant Rebekah wouldn't be getting home to Mike and the girls.

She cursed her idiocy at agreeing to go into work the day before Christmas Eve, cursed her boss, Quentin, for being the money-grabbing, heartless bastard that he was.

It wasn't like the wife-cheating, upper-class 'wannabe' with his expensive BMW and manor house off near Chard needed the bloody money, flogging his poor workers like some modern-day Scrooge so he could jet off to the Bahamas every six months.

Rebekah cursed the relentless, god-damn snow and

Christmas as well, muttering disparagingly under her breath about the whole bloody lot of it.

Rebekah cowered trembling around the corner, cupping her hands around her cigarette as she tried desperately to light it, the wind beginning to howl fiercely. The hood of her parka coat billowed round her head, her lengthy, jet-black hair fluttering around her cold face as she turned against the wind, leaning against the marble pillar outside her office's front door. She knew she only had herself to blame for being out in this bloody snow-storm but she needed a cigarette badly, it had been an unproductive morning, punctuated by frequent phone-calls from Quentin that annoyed more than assisted.

Her colleague, Hannah, had laughed at her when Rebekah had said she was going outside for a cigarette, calling her a lunatic, shaking her head like some old school ma'am and tutting.

Then had laughed that infectious laugh of hers which had set Rebekah off.

They had called each other some rather unsavoury and unflattering names in an exchange that reminded Rebekah of those out-takes at the end of Liar, Liar, Rebekah's favourite film of all time. She was forever quoting it, forever impersonating Jim Carrey delivering those funny lines. She'd slip into Ace Ventura territory every now and again, which would invariably lead into a passable Austin Powers impersonation and Hannah would always laugh uncontrollably.

Goldmember was her favourite film.

Mike was the master though, his uncanny knack for mimicry and recollection of film quotes was part of the reason Rebekah loved him so.

That and the fact he worshipped the ground she walked on.

He hadn't been happy that Quentin had called her in, especially the day before Christmas Eve, especially when Oakleigh was suffering from its worse winter for nearly fifty years.

But he hadn't laboured the point, he'd told her to hurry home and that the girls would be OK, had even offered to walk in and meet her with the girls and the dog.

Rebekah had said that she'd let him know.

Rebekah had promised to make it up to him later, Mike's eyes had widened, he'd had a salacious grin on his face while doing his best impersonation of Groucho Marx with the wriggling eyebrows.

Rebekah had smacked his bottom and kissed him goodbye, tutting and shaking her head as she'd left.

That made her smile to herself as she drew heavily upon her cigarette, coughing madly as the wind caught the smoke in her throat and threatened to choke her in the snow.

She pitched the cigarette butt into the wind and watched it catch it and take it twenty feet away, clearing the other side of the road with ease.

Oakleigh's Main Street, the central street that ran through the town centre was completely deserted. Most of the shops were closed, most other businesses were closed, even The Hangman's Arms and The Griffon, the two public houses at either end of Main Street, were seemingly in darkness, though from that angle she couldn't really make out too much.

And yet, it was only 1 pm.

On a Thursday afternoon.

Further up the street, toward The Hangman's Arms, on the opposite side of the road, Rebekah could see that the small, independent book shop, 'Cookin' The Books' had its main light on but tellingly, the large Waterstones opposite was completely dark. Annie Cook, the quirky, yet lovely, owner and manageress of the small book shop was one of Oakleigh's nicest shop-keepers and would open come hell or high water.

Rebekah doubted anyone would be entering her store

today. Or whether anyone had for a long time, if she was honest.

Rebekah pulled the front of her Parka tighter across her chest and thrust her hands deep into it's pockets as she used her shoulder to push open the office building's heavy door and stepped back inside.

Shivering and shaking the snow from her hair, she slipped off her coat as she re-entered the small office, Hannah deep in conversation with someone on the end of her mobile phone-line, playfully flipping Rebekah the finger.

Rebekah replied in kind, using both hands, before sitting back down at her desk.

She grabbed her clutch-bag and fished out her iPhone, swiping across with one finger, to unlock it and checked if she'd had any messages.

She hadn't.

She thought about giving Mike a quick ring, just to let him know she was still alive, that hadn't frozen to death in this ice-box of an office and that she would still cut Quentin's balls off if the bastard had dared to show his face that god-awful day.

She decided it could wait.

Hannah was obviously talking to her husband, Ollie, judging by amount of times she called whoever 'babe', 'honey' and once, unnervingly, 'Mr Big'.

Rebekah stifled a laugh and flicked back on her computer monitor.

It was then she had that feeling that someone was watching her, that creeping sensation that made the hair on the back of her neck stand up and goosebumps form upon her forearms.

Looking out of the small office window that overlooked her desk, Rebekah saw someone standing on the other side of the road, seemingly looking straight at her.

A Father Christmas, resplendent in the traditional red

coat with white trim, red trousers, jet black boots with the whitest, longest beard she had ever seen, was staring at her.

He was stood completely still, the wind and snow barely making his robe move at all and Rebekah was convinced he was looking directly at her.

She looked around at Hannah who was toying with her gold necklace as she swirled around upon her swivel-chair, laughing at whoever was on the other end of her phone-call.

Looking back, she expected to see the Father Christmas was gone.

He was ominously still there.

Rebekah motioned with her hand, flapping it wildly, trying to grab Hannah's attention while she stared at the person standing on the other side of the road.

Hannah caught sight of Rebekah's gesticulations and slid over, her chair gliding across the laminate flooring as if on ice.

Rebekah looked at Hannah for a split second as she crashed into Rebekah's chair, giggling as they skidded together, her big boobs squashing against Rebekah's arm which made Hannah laugh more.

Rebekah expected the jolly fellow to have disappeared, as if she was in some crappy, cheap horror film and no one can see the bad guy except for the damsel in distress.

He was still there.

Hannah told Ollie that she had to go then peered at the person standing on the other side of the street, squinting through her drooping eyelids.

"Ho-Fucking-Ho!" Hannah laughed, "Santa has come early!"

"I just looked up and could see him staring in at me. Fucking creepy!"

Hannah stood up, banged defiantly upon the window and stuck her middle finger up at the person stood opposite.

"Fuck off Santa!" she yelled with a laugh, though knew he couldn't hear her anyway. "Was he out there when you went for your fag?"

Rebekah shook her head.

"The street was deserted, only dickheads would be out in weather like that."

Hannah laughed, giving her a withering look that said 'I know, love, I know.'

The two of them looked back out of the window and the Father Christmas had gone.

"Looks like your finger scared him off." Rebekah laughed nervously, still a little shaken by what she assumed was some weirdo staring at her.

"Well, if I get butchered on my walk home tonight, then you know the jolly, fat fucker was really pissed off at me! No chance for me to get off the 'Naughty List' this year then!"

Rebekah scolded her, gently slapping Hannah on her upper arm, which made Hannah feign pain, cry out, then howl with laughter as she sat back down in her chair and slid back across to her own desk.

Rebekah shivered involuntarily, partly because of the coldness of the room because despite wearing a thermal vest, a white blouse, thick woollen jumper and a scarf, the office was damn freezing.

And partly because she instinctively knew that guy, dressed as Father Christmas, had definitely been watching her, standing perfectly still in the wind and snow.

Hannah obviously wasn't a) concerned by the cold, wearing a low-cut blouse that left little to the imagination or b) overtly concerned by some guy ogling her best friend. She sat in her chair, singing a Christmas song, swinging her hips from side to side as if she hadn't a care in the world.

Rebekah sighed and continued with her work, despite feeling just a little sleepy now, thinking about the long walk home in a few hours, hoping that the snow would stop falling.

And hoping that nothing would happen to her before she got home.

At a little after 4.30pm, Hannah leaped up from her chair, switched off her computer and reached for her bright yellow, padded winter coat that was hung upon the old-fashioned, wooden hat-stand by the front door.

"Time to get the fuck out of here, my dear!" she laughed, wrapping her woollen scarf multiple times around her neck, untangling her flowing blonde tresses from her collar.

Rebekah didn't need telling twice.

She repeated Hannah's leaving routine, computer off, coat and scarf on, unhooking her black hair and shaking it loose.

The two of them left the office after Hannah had switched off the main lights and armed the security alarm, the two of them arm in arm as they opened the door and stepped out into the evening.

Darkness had started to fall, the snow flurries relenting slightly as the wind turned into a cold breeze, the thick snow laying all around them like a freshly fallen, silent shroud.

Rebekah heard 'I Am A Rock' by Simon and Garfunkel somewhere in the back of her mind and smiled at her own cleverness at such an image.

Hannah was singing 'Let It Snow' under her breath, grinning like the cat who got the cream.

"Cheerful bitch!" Rebekah tutted.

Hannah kissed her on the cheek, burying her face into the soft padding of her own coat.

"It's Christmas!" Hannah shouted at the top of her voice, her rasping, unnervingly accurate impersonation of Slade's Noddy Holder splitting the silence of the cold, evening air, echoing through the deserted Main Street.

Rebekah shook her head, smiling at her best friend's

festive cheer, hoping that no one had been there to hear such an ear-shattering scream.

Or indeed, been watching them from the other side of the street.

Dressed like Father Christmas, or otherwise.

She furtively glanced all around discreetly while Hannah burst into song, singing the chorus of Slade's 'Merry Christmas Everyone'.

There was no sign of any brightly coloured, fat, jovial fellow, or indeed any sign of anyone else around at all, all the shops, all the buildings were dark.

Luckily the town council had gone overboard with the lights and decorations, making the street resemble Santa's Grotto. There were reds, golds and greens adorning shop windows, balustrades, balcony's, rows upon rows of festive lights as far as the eye could see, dozens of Christmas trees lining the street, one upon each building.

Luckily, the blazing lights illuminated the town as darkness fell.

"Drink before home?" Hannah indicated where by a nod of her head in the direction of The Hangman's Arms, up the street.

Rebekah looked at Hannah and shook her head.

"Want to get home before it gets any darker. Crossing that bloody bridge is bad enough with this bloody snow during the day, let alone in the bloody dark."

"Should have brought your car today!"

Rebekah fought the urge not to punch Hannah on the arm again, harder and more purposefully this time.

Despite owning a 4×4 that was lovingly referred as her 'Yummy Mummy Tractor', Rebekah had been unable to drive in that day as Mike had been unable to get it started, or dig it out from the ten-foot snow drift that had buried it outside their farmhouse.

Reluctantly she'd had to walk into Oakleigh, maybe only a mile and a half from their farm on the south side of the town but far enough when the snow was piled so high and there seemed to be no end to it falling.

It may have been a little tough going but at least the terrain was flat, the gradient wasn't too steep and in the morning it had looked picturesque, to say the least.

With it starting to get dark, it probably wouldn't be such a nice walk home though.

And she wished that Mike had made good on his offer to meet her.

"You want me to walk you home, sweetheart?"

Rebekah pondered Hannah's offer for second then shook her head.

"Nah, you're OK sweetie. It's the opposite direction for you. You get going."

Hannah kissed her on the cheek then threw her arms around her, pulling her in for a bear-hug that threatened to break Rebekah's back.

"You have a fantastic Christmas bestie! Give me a ring on Christmas Day, let me speak to those gorgeous god-children of mine."

Rebekah nodded, barely able to breath as Hannah held on for dear life, then burst into laughter as Hannah pulled her face into her welcoming bosom and made her 'motorboat' her.

"Nutcase!" Rebekah shouted when she was finally let up for air and sent on her merry way with a loud, painful slap from Hannah across her butt-cheek, luckily partly deflected by the hem of her parka coat.

Hannah waved cheerfully as she walked toward the corner of Bodley Street, grinning madly and singing her Christmas songs as she went.

Rebekah, pulled up her coat's hood, thrust her hands deep into the pockets of her parka and set off for home, Hannah's singing floating down to her upon the now-gentle breeze.

Then she heard Hannah scream

Rebekah spun around, too quick for her coat so she had to push it from her face.

She saw Hannah, twenty feet away, right at the corner of Bodley Street where it met Main Street laughing her head off, laying upon her back in a small snow-drift, flailing her arms and legs around wildly.

"Fucking Snow Angels!" Hannah squealed, "Merry Christmas honey!"

Rebekah shook her head in mock-disbelief, muttering to herself about the sanity of her dearest and oldest friend as she turned away and set off for home.

Laughing to herself, Hannah lay there looking up at the grey sky, small flakes of snow still falling all over her, all around her and continued on swiping her arms and legs to create a bigger snow angel. She was glad she had given Rebekah one last laugh before they had separated, she had looked so on edge after seeing that Santa earlier.

God knew why though. It was hardly surprising that someone in this shitty, little town had decided to join in the festivities and dress up as the big red guy. Or that they would want to look at the two sexiest women still at work in the town centre.

But staring at them was possibly not the best way to attract a woman, no matter how accommodating or festive they were particularly feeling.

Still, he had fucked off pretty sharpish when she had flipped him 'the bird' and that still made her smile.

No one fucked with Hannah and her 'sister'.

There was not a lot that scared her, if she was honest, she'd had her share of arseholes in her life and did not suffer fools gladly. People only saw, the sexy clothes, the red lipstick and the rather big boobs but there was so much more to her than that. She would kill to protect any of her friends, she had a very strong moral code that she had always stood by defiantly.

People called her 'ballsy', strong-willed, a cougar long before its connotations had been forever changed to something far more salacious.

'TIS THE SEASON

She was 45 going on 21 and loving life.

Dragging herself up onto her elbows, Hannah watched her dark-haired, beautiful friend go trudging off through the snow and smiled to herself.

She hoped she would get home quickly and that the snow wouldn't slow her down too much.

Hannah got to her feet, wiped the excess snow from her padded jacket and stomped her feet, her black, thigh-length boots shedding the same snow.

Darkness was falling far too quick so she turned to head off for home.

Standing in the doorway of the corner house, half-hidden in the shadows, Father Christmas stepped forward, making her cry out.

"Fuck me!" Hannah laughed, "you scared the shit out of me!"

Father Christmas never said a word, blue eyes staring at her from behind the thicket of a huge, white beard.

"So Santa, got anything in your sack for li'l old me?"

He still never uttered a word.

Hannah, feeling a little aggrieved that this bastard seemed to be ignoring her, started to walk around the doorway.

Father Christmas stepped down from the doorstep, blocking her way.

"Look," she sighed, anger beginning to sound in her normally-calm voice, "it's been a long day, I've finished for the Christmas period and I'm going home. Have a Merry Christmas and get the fuck out of my way."

A white gloved hand shot out and grabbed her by her scarf, yanking her forward.

Hannah opened her mouth to cry out but his other hand enveloped her face as she was propelled forward and the last she experienced was the over-powering smell of mince pies, holly and sherry before darkness greeted her like an old friend.

Rebekah walked as quickly as she could through the snow drifts that lined the pavements, occasionally stepping into road where the snow had been compacted down over the past few days.

The wind had picked up slightly so she had put her head down but could still catch sight of the brightly lit windows of the houses at the bottom of Main Street as she crossed at the large roundabout and turned into Kings Road. King's Road gave way to Lower Bridge Road, Hannah knowing that within ten minutes she'd be at the bridge that traversed the river, then ten minutes from home.

Home to Upton Farm where Mike and the girls were patiently awaiting her arrival with a roaring log fire, chestnuts hopefully roasting and mulled wine gently simmering upon the log-burner.

This warmed her nearly as much as her energetic walk to get there.

More than once, she thought she heard sleigh-bells carried on the cold breeze which made her stop but it was Christmas, no doubt families were playing Christmas songs behind their closed doors, so it was hardly surprising.

Rebekah loved this time of the year, loved the warm glow inside that festivities gave her. She loved the songs, the decorations, the time of family togetherness.

But having a staring Father Christmas had seriously freaked her out.

Again, it was probably unsurprising that someone had decided to dress that way but it had been the way he had been looking directly at her for such a long time, right outside her office window.

At least he hadn't been dressed like the Grim Reaper.

She laughed to herself at the thought of that image because whenever she saw it, she always thought of Death in 'Family Guy', or The Ghost Of Christmas Future from another of her beloved Christmas films 'Scrooged'.

Still, that Father Christmas, no matter how jovial he

was meant to be, how brightly his white beard shone, how bright his colourful costume had been, had still unnerved her.

It was almost laughable that the symbol of all the season of peace and goodwill to all men had scared her.

But there was something wrong with the way he had just stood there.

Rebekah took a reluctant peek over her shoulder, half expecting to see big, fat, jolly Father Christmas walking down the road behind her.

He wasn't.

King's Road was as deserted as Main Street had been, flanked with buried cars that looked like huge boulders covered in a white blanket of snow. The street-lights gave the area an eerie, yellow tinge, sprinkled with the occasional blinking Fairy light that twinkled from the row of dark houses.

But there was no Father Christmas, neither standing, leering at her or menacingly following her.

She pressed on towards Lower Bridge Road, the wind beginning to pick up once more as the bridge came into view.

Rebekah walked as quickly as the snow would let her, her boots sinking deep in the drifts with each laboured, strength-sapping step towards home.

As the road flattened out, Lower Oakleigh Bridge loomed in the gloom, it's crumbling, ham-stone hidden beneath the white blanket, the soft, steady rumble of the river becoming louder as she approached.

It was then she saw a figure stood in the middle of the bridge, feint in the swirling snow as if on the periphery of her vision.

It was someone dressed like Father Christmas.

And carrying a mammoth sack upon their back.

Rebekah raised her hand to shield her eyes as the snow billowed and buffeted her as she stumbled forward.

Father Christmas threw his sack down upon the

ground and shook it empty.

Rebekah could have sworn that a body had been unceremoniously tipped out upon the snow-covered bridge.

Her scream got carried away upon the gusting wind that kicked up more flurries around her, and she broke into a run as the Father Christmas bent down over the fallen figure at his feet.

Hannah.

Rebekah, without any care or concern for her own safety, was running ungainly, haphazardly, at danger of falling at any moment, onto the bridge toward her fallen friend.

Father Christmas lifted Hannah off of the ground by her throat and as Rebekah fell short by five feet before him, skidding face-first into the cold, deep snow, he threw her lifeless body over the side of the bridge.

Rebekah, screaming half in horror, half in sheer frustration, watched her friend disappear over the side, watching her blonde hair billowing around her, hearing her body hit the water.

Dragging herself to her feet, Rebekah realised that Father Christmas was looking straight at her, his hands on his considerable hips, piercing, cobalt-blue eyes staring deep into hers.

She could have sworn his shoulders were moving, believing without a shadow of a doubt that he was laughing.

Or at the very least saying, 'Ho-Ho-Ho.'

She put her head down and ran at him, adrenaline and pure venomous rage blowing away any notions of self-preservation or terrifying danger.

Despite the short distance between them, Rebekah stumbled as she ran, her Wellington boots catching in a particularly hard patch of snow and sending her sprawling before she could connect with the Father Christmas.

The bridge was empty.

'TIS THE SEASON

Rebekah skidded to a halt by the side of the bridge, face first into a snow-drift that stopped her from smashing her face into the sandy-coloured rocks.

Clumsily, she pulled herself up and frantically scanned the side of the bridge, praying for a glimpse of Hannah, or what she hoped with all her heart, wasn't Hannah.

The black river, as dark as night, flowed noisily beneath her, a swirling rumble of nothingness beneath where she propped herself.

She once again had the feeling that there was something looking at her and glancing across to the far side of the bridge, twenty feet away stood the Father Christmas figure.

Standing between her and the lane that led to her home.

"Where is Hannah, you bastard?" Rebekah screamed shrilly, "what have you done with her?"

The sound of his 'Ho-Ho-Ho' would haunt her for the rest of her life.

It was guttural, dank and dirty, almost demonic, sounding like it was being drawn across a million razor-blades, sounding like it had come from the very depths of hell itself.

From behind her, from the other end of the bridge closest to town, Rebekah heard what sounded like jingling bells once more. Only this time, it was closer, louder.

There, stumbling towards her, like one of those stupid zombies from The Walking Dead that Mike absolutely adored, was Hannah.

Hannah, wearing what looked for all the world like some whore's version of a naughty elf, boobs half hanging out, a skimpy, barely adequate mini-skirt that showed far too much leg and crotch.

And a crooked green hat perched upon her masses of blonde, bouncy ringlets.

Her face, as pale as the snow that law all around, was

splattered with what Rebekah assumed could only be blood, in the shape of a hand-print that covered from brow to chin.

There looked like blood all down her front, upon her mesh-stocking covered legs, on her small, white ankle-boots.

"IT'S CHRISTMAS!" Hannah screamed, her voice sounding gargled as if she was speaking with her mouth full, "HAVE I GOT A FUCKING PRESENT FOR YOOOOOOOU!"

Rebekah scurried away on her backside, trying to put as much distance from her and 'Hannah' as possible with her back to the raging river behind her, fear streaking up her spine like a bullet from a gun.

The Father Christmas, still laughing his malevolent Christmas refrain, turned and started to walk toward the country lane that led to the farmhouse, disappearing into the darkness beyond, the snow still swirling all around.

Rebekah looked back to see that Hannah was now right beside her, looming upon her like a jump-scare in some tacky horror film.

Rebekah screamed nonetheless.

Hannah laughed; a throaty, deliciously dirty laugh that spat droplets of blood in Rebekah's face.

"Here's your present!" she hissed, a shit-eating grin on her face that reminded Rebekah of Pennywise from Stephen King's 'It'.

And with both bloodied hands, shoved Rebekah violently backwards.

Rebekah saw the world spin upside down, tumbling backwards over the edge of the bridge, a cry of horror escaping from her open mouth like a bat out of hell, waiting for her to plunge into the icy river below.

Rebekah banged her head upon the rough carpet, the swivel chair tangled in her sprawled legs, Hannah's laughter ringing in her ears.

Her eyes flicked open and her friend was sat in her own chair, laughing that infectious, yet child-like laugh of hers which Rebekah usually found most endearing.

She didn't at that precise moment in time.

"I watched you," Hannah sniggered, "watched your eyes falling closed, literally in time with you leaning further and further back on your chair. Fucking hysterical!"

"Do you think you can stop laughing enough to help me up you bitch?"

That made Hannah laugh more.

With her giggling friend's assistance, Rebekah got to her feet and right-sided her office chair, patting herself down for comic effect as if she was covered in a shit-ton of dust and debris.

"That was worth coming In the day before Christmas Eve," Hannah laughed and Rebekah knew that it wasn't going to go away any time soon; the laughter or the story of how she fell asleep and fell off her chair.

Rebekah sat back down in her chair and pulled it tightly up to her desk, smiling to herself.

Then she raised her head to look out of the window directly ahead of her.

There was five Father Christmas' staring directly at her.

Rebekah's hand went to her mouth, her breath catching in her throat as she stifled a scream.

Then the five started hollering, waving like demented loons, their cat-calls and wolf-whistles faint through the glazed window, a couple of them gyrating their loins seductively in her direction.

These 'Father Christmas' wore shoddy, tattered and food-stained outfits, their false beards slipping from their faces, the bottles of imported lager held aloft in waving, glove-less hands.

"Bloody footballers!" Hannah laughed, suddenly appearing at Rebekah's shoulder which made her jump a little, "that's Ryan Bagwell and his cronies. I'd recognise his beer-gut and small bulge anywhere!"

Hannah stuck her middle fingers up at the men, a shiver running down Rebekah's spine as she recalled the last time she had done the same thing.

The men shouted and cheered louder as Hannah mouthed the words "fuck off!" at them all, still grinning that winning mile of hers.

"Bunch of dickheads!" Hannah laughed, playfully punching Rebekah softly upon the upper arm, "they like you though!"

Rebekah sighed, finally letting calm take hold once again, breathing a little easier as the men went on their merry way and saw other hardy pedestrians navigating the treacherous, snow-covered pavements.

The street outside, still looking like a Victorian Christmas card, weren't as quiet as she'd previously encountered but there was still something a little unsettling about very few people out in about in Oakleigh.

She looked at the clock upon the wall.

It was 2pm.

Her doze had only lasted about ten minutes but she decided that she wouldn't be venturing outside for a cigarette any time soon. She'd wait until home time.

At a little before 5pm, Hannah let out a laboured cry as she stretched in her swivel chair, her arms high above her head, arching her back and thrusting her chest out almost as if she was Jennifer Beals in 'Flashdance'.

"That's it!" she shouted, "time to do what one shepherd said to the other shepherd."

"Get the flock out of here?" Rebekah replied, laughing at their shared joke at the line from Lethal Weapon.

Hannah was up and out of her chair, reaching for her big, yellow, padded jacket and woollen scarf.

"You bet yer arse, sister!" Hannah laughed, reaching for her large handbag that she had stored under her desk,

"Hannah is on a promise this evening, hubby wants his present early!"

Rebekah knew what Hannah meant and wasn't going to get drawn on her best friend's plan for any sexual shenanigans for that evening. She wasn't a prude and god knew Hannah wasn't, Rebekah just had enough of her tales of uninterrupted, childless love-making to last her for that year.

The pair of them alarmed the office and made their way out through the double doors, Hannah jabbering away at ten to the dozen. About how great Ollie was, how frequently he did her, his size, length and girth, all information that Rebekah could have done without being told. But she laughed along nonetheless.

Hannah, not looking where she was going as usual, ploughed through the open door and straight into Mike, who stood his ground and let her bounce off of him, grinning like a naughty school-boy.

"All right Hooter McBoobs?" he laughed, giving Rebekah a cheeky, yet knowing wink, "good job you've got such great padding, you could have done yourself a real mischief there!"

Hannah's playful punch caught Mike full in the chest and hurt him a lot more than he let on but he laughed long and hard nonetheless, wrapping an affectionate arm around her.

Rebekah bent down and swept her waiting girls up into her arms, hugging the pair of them as tight as humanly possible, their whoops of delight ringing in her ears as she buried her face between them. Her relief at seeing them both and Mike was palpable, though she tried her hardest not to let it show that much.

She failed.

"What's up honey?" Mike sighed, kissing her tenderly upon her cheek, "you look a little jaded."

"Great chat-up line Mister!" Hannah laughed, ruffling both the girl's hair.

"I'm OK. Just a little tired. Am just glad to see you guys."

The family's black Labrador, Max, bounded around them excitedly, obviously pleased to be with them and out and about in the deep snow.

Rebekah made a fuss of him too, bending down to stroke behind his ear as she set the girls down.

"Right, this sickly tableau of family goodness has made me crave alcohol so I bid you lovely people adieu! Have a great Christmas guys, will call day after tomorrow."

Hannah kissed them all in turn, giving Rebekah a huge hug and smacking Mike upon the backside.

And with that, Hannah strode purposefully up the road, marching through the rising snow.

Singing 'Merry Christmas Everybody' at the top of her voice as she went.

Rebekah watched her best friend walking away and shuddered.

Especially when she saw the group of footballers dressed as Father Christmas were coming out of The Hangman's Arms, obviously the worse for wear and being rather loud.

Hannah, still singing, deftly crossed the road to avoid them, ignoring their lecherous catcalls and wolf-whistles until level with them and then curtseyed over-dramatically.

That made them whoop louder, their good-natured banter loud enough to make Rebekah blush for her children but her girls were too busy throwing snowballs at each other to take any notice.

"Let's get going honey."

Mike nodded, smiling, calling for the girls to come closer before they set off on their way home.

Rebekah glanced over her shoulder, to check on Hannah for the last time before she disappeared around the corner, looking to see the rowdy Father Christmas' had moved off, still sending salacious comments Hannah's way.

One of them was stood a few feet away from the others, looking Rebekah's way, the opposite of the others. This one wore a more accurate outfit, a better fitting outfit.

"Everything alright honey?"

Rebekah looked at her husband and smiled.

"Yeah, just making sure Hannah is OK."

She looked back and Hannah had disappeared around the corner.

And the Father Christmas was gone.

Rebekah listened to Mike putting the girls to bed, Max curled up around her feet as she sipped from a large glass of mulled wine. The log-fire was roaring, giving their living room a warm glow as the snow storm raged outside, the wind whistling around the outside of the farm-house.

She had slipped on her pyjamas, her thick towelling robe and her novelty 'Hairy Monster Feet' slippers and sat upon the cloth-covered settee, her hair still a little damp from her relaxing bath earlier.

The satellite TV signal had gone down half an hour earlier so reluctantly she'd put on her Amazon Echo and was now listening to Michael Buble's Christmas album, his soft dulcet tones filling the room.

Mike was reading the girls a bed-time story, his deep voice filtering down the stony staircase, making Rebekah smile at his animated retelling of a Christmas story.

Max raised his head, sniffing the air then there came a low growl from the back of his throat, his hackles beginning to rise.

Rebekah looked up and thought she saw movement in the crack of the closed curtains behind the illuminated, overly-decorated Christmas tree.

She almost cried out as her heart leapt into her mouth, spilling her glass of wine a little.

Max continued to growl.

Mike appeared at the top of the stairs.

"What's the matter with Max?"

Rebekah placed her near-empty glass upon the lamp-table beside the sofa and unfurled her legs from under the dog.

"I think there's someone outside."

Her voice was little more than a whisper, barely audible above Michael's crooning.

Mike peered out of the landing window, craning his neck to look down above the large oaken front door.

"Looks like carol singers! Mad buggers out this kind of night!" he laughed, "Max obviously has better hearing than us. And more taste. I'll get rid of them."

Mike walked downstairs, walking towards the front door before Rebekah could say a word.

She wanted to protest, wanted to tell him to get the shotgun from the locked gun-box under the stairs, wanted him to stay away from the door.

Wanted him not to open the door.

Mike opened it before she had a chance.

Rebekah, slowly moving up off the sofa as if she was moving underwater, her mouth opening laggardly as her words took an eternity to come forth.

Mike's smile faded as he came face to face with four pale, haggard, thin men and women, all wearing what appeared to be Christmas fancy dress.

All four of them covered in what could only be described as blood.

Then Rebekah's blood ran cold as she heard both her daughter's excited squeals of delight from up in their room, their laughter filling the air.

"Mum, Dad!" they shouted, "Father Christmas has come early! He's standing outside our window. He's shouting 'Ho-Ho-Ho'!!!"

'TIS THE SEASON

AFTERWORD

Each story in this collection of short stories can be read separately, they can be read in any order, they only have the fictional town of Oakleigh in common (though a few characters and situations may inexplicably rear their ugly heads elsewhere, cheeky bastards!)

Oakleigh is absolutely NOT Chard (Mr Bagg, I'm looking at you!) and I have tried to make it as obvious and as plain as I can, to the extent that I have said some rather scurrilous things about my home town, within the story 'Heaven Or Hell' to illustrate the differences.

These views, however off-kilter and off-colour they may be, are all my own and have to be taken with an extremely large pinch of salt...like some of the characters in these stories, I love my home town to a fault, however it may come across in what I've written. Chard is definitely a much better town than a lot of people give it credit and in all honesty its no better and no worse than a lot of towns throughout this glorious little island. Even if some of the people in it think and say otherwise.

But Oakleigh….Oakleigh is hell on earth...literally.

A lot of writers have created their own towns throughout their careers and the most obvious for people who know me, would be Stephen King (with Derry & Castle Rock to name a couple) but its not exclusive to him, many authors create somewhere new.

So for those who will say "Oh, delusions of grandeur AGAIN" and "oh God, he STILL thinks he's Stephen King!" I think you'll find its a lot more common than you realise. It was just easier for me to imagine a new town, next door to my own that gave me license to do what the hell I liked.

I know some of the stories enclosed in this collection may frustrate the reader, some creating more questions than answers, some leaving you hanging.

But like, On The Outside, I may revisit some stories, some situations at a later date. That's the joy of writing, a story is never truly finished, never done and dusted and I'm sure there is more out there for the people of that weird and wonderful little town.

I must thank all those extremely kind souls who bought On The Outside, both e-book and paperback copies, those three even kinder souls that gave it a review on Amazon (reviews sell more books apparently, so hit me up if you can!). I also must thank each and every person who offered me an opinion on that book, asked when the next one was coming out and have taken an interest in what I have written or what I am going to write. You may not believe me when I say that I'm not in this for fame and money but I genuinely enjoy writing (always have!) and to have people take an interest in that is extremely humbling and heart-warming.

I thank you all.

Suffice to say, there will be more from this author; some may say good stories, some may say not so good but I will keep churning out stories just the same.

Again, none of this would be possible without the unwavering support and belief of both my family and friends, some that I have mentioned before, some that I haven't. You all know who you are, this book is for all of you.

Justin Mason
Chard, Somerset
October 2018

Printed in Poland
by Amazon Fulfillment
Poland Sp. z o.o., Wrocław